THE MYSTERY AT RAKE HALL

THE MYSTERY
AT RAKE HALL

C.S. Lewis Investigates

Maureen Paton

Swift

SWIFT PRESS

First published in Great Britain by Swift Press 2025

1 3 5 7 9 8 6 4 2

Printed and bound in Great Britain by CPI Group (UK) Ltd,
Croydon CRO 4YY

A CIP catalogue record for this book is available from the
British Library

We make every effort to make sure our products are safe for the purpose
for which they are intended. Our authorised representative in the EU for
product safety is Easy Access System Europe, Mustamäe tee 50,
10621 Tallinn, Estonia gpsr.requests@easproject.com

ISBN: 9781800754836
eISBN: 9781800754843

In memory of my mother, Blanche

THE MYSTERY AT RAKE HALL

AUTUMN 1947

CHAPTER 1

Normally, he never took much notice of what a female student was wearing. That way danger lay, even if you were saying something gallant about their outfit. And Jack Lewis wasn't that kind of man. But there had been something odd about Susan Temple's appearance at tutorials recently that had puzzled him, try though he might to set his mind on higher things.

And now, for the second week in a row, there was no sign of her. Tapping his pipe on his desk to give himself time to ponder, he eventually looked up at the long, glum face of the other pupil, Christopher Henchard, who was probably also wondering why Temple hadn't turned up to help him out of his usual scholarly jam with some well-chosen words.

Although she looked as delicate and willowy as one of the wood nymphs from Lewis's beloved Greek mythology, Temple stood up well to intellectual interrogation. There was something defiant about her that amused him; despite his college image as a middle-aged bachelor terrified of what the university's young bucks called 'totty', he secretly relished pitching his wits against the women students. Having fought to gain admission in the first place to the tiny minority of female colleges, they were almost guaranteed to be brighter than many of the men – especially the rugger buggers heading for thirds after spending too much time on the pitch. Lewis, a clumsy, butterfingered man, detested sport and left all that to his brother Warnie.

Yet the vulnerability of someone as rashly combative as Temple also disturbed him. There were men who would see that as a challenge and take advantage – especially with her lush-lipped, high-cheekboned, dark beauty, although he tried not to be too aware of that. He had always been bothered by the potential susceptibility of the female undergrads, so vastly outnumbered by their male counterparts after leaving home for the first time – and therefore only too ripe for exploitation and domination.

The don knew he was being patronising – tantamount to suggesting that they were the weaker sex, not up to the demands of academia, which was certainly not his intention – yet it troubled him nonetheless. After all, the university had yet to recover from the strange and shocking case of the girl who had been found dead in her bed in Lady Margaret Hall only the previous term. The inquest had established that she had a weak heart, a condition confirmed by her family, yet the whisper was that she had been taking amphetamines to cram overnight for her finals.

Benzedrine tablets, or Bennies, were technically not illegal: the RAF boys had been chucking them down their throats to match the Luftwaffe's daily doses of Pervitin for the bloody dogfights of war. But not for nothing were amphetamines nicknamed 'speed', and the jury was still out on their effect on a dodgy ticker – or even on a normal one.

Where had she got the stuff? A boyfriend had to be involved, according to the usual order of things in which young women were led on by worldlier men. Not all of them were callow youths of the same age as the girls: a number of male students had deferred their higher education in order to serve in the war. And when they returned from the conflict, these soldier-students were sometimes damaged men, just like the don himself after the First World War. Most of them had been officers, but they were not necessarily gentlemen.

Beyond that was the lurking presence of black marketeers, whose dabs were over everything in this and every other city. They seemed to exert an unhealthy influence over students with more money than sense – of which there were far too many, in Lewis's opinion.

According to the university grapevine, the pathologist had found no evidence of substances in the girl's body, but it might all have been hushed up to prevent a scandal. The official verdict was accidental death, much to the relief of the college, as well as her distraught parents. The local papers covered it as a nib, a 'news in brief'. But the tantalisingly short reports continued to haunt Lewis, a details man. He remembered how he had once over-heard a bunch of Senior Common Room sherry gossips smack-ing their lips while piously shaking their heads over the dead girl's 'parchment-pale' face. He found it hard to stomach the gloating interest; it was as if they were old dears sharing hospital horrors over the garden fence. But then these were men that had never been war-forged.

His thoughts returned to the strangely absent Susan Temple. Of course, it was never the done thing to chase up students if they didn't turn up for seminars or tutorials; that was their look-out. There was usually a reckoning at the end of each term with questions asked about gaps in attendance if they affected their performance, but great universities were not schools, and under-graduates were not children. At this level, they were expected to be self-disciplined, which was why higher education could be so overwhelming for the weaker students.

Susan Temple was not one of them. If she was unwell, the usual form was to send a note with an excuse, but no apology had arrived. Usually, she showed up early to show off with her latest essay, a smile on her face at the certainty of impressing the exacting Mr Lewis yet again.

He knew he would have to contact Somerville and her other tutors eventually, but he was reluctant to cry wolf too soon and perhaps get the girl into trouble. It seemed to him that Temple was too clever to stage a disappearing act without a very good reason.

'Grim day, sir,' said the clearly hung-over Henchard, trying to delay the dreaded business of reading out his meandering thoughts on Spenser.

This term, his written work had not been quite so lazy and patchy as usual, and Lewis, who had one of the finest noses in the university for sniffing out deceit, suspected the involvement of another hand. The subtlest of touches, of course, to try to conceal the spectral presence of a ghostwriter, usually one of the better students.

Could that be behind Temple's non-appearance? She might be reluctant to look him in the eye; she could get sent down as well as Henchard if she were found to be helping him, especially for payment. Yet judging by what Lewis had observed, she was much more the type to brazen things out.

Spears of horizontal rain were being hurled by an angry weather god at the windows of the chaotic sitting room where the detritus from yesterday's afternoon tea – Lewis's favourite meal, a hang-over from his nursery days – sat on top of piles of paper. The lino was scratched and singed in places, a cheap floor-covering that did no favours to the handsome white-panelled room with its perfect view of the college's Grove meadow.

His tiny book-stacked study and bedroom faced in the opposite direction on to Magdalen's tranquil Cloisters and Tower, but so long as there was enough fuel to warm the bigger room, the don preferred that hint of wildness outside a window. The Grove reminded him of the wood behind The Kilns, his house in nearby Headington, that gave its grounds what he imagined was a certain epic quality. Sometimes he thought that a thousand sinister golden eyes were fixed upon him as he looked out. It was only the deer sheltering in the bracken, yet he put the feeling of paranoia down to the wartime surveillance that seemed to have continued into peacetime.

The never-ending shortages encouraged people to spy on each other, always wondering who might be concealing a secret stash supplied by the ugly, prowling profiteers. Some of those creatures were known as 'claw boys', according to gossip passed on by his own loyal Magdalen servant Cyril, known as Squirrel. When Squirrel told Lewis they derived the nickname from the razor blades they used as weapons, it was hard to suppress a shudder. 'Surely they would never dare in somewhere like Oxford? Maybe parts of London, but not here?' Squirrel merely tapped his nose, glad to have passed on the warning just in case. Not that saintly Mr Lewis was ever likely to be in danger from such a source.

When the don's domestic slavery at The Kilns allowed, he particularly liked to linger by one of the old stone-quarry pools between the house's nearby trees. Sometimes he tried to take a punt out, but the almighty effort with the pole was usually defeated by his physical awkwardness. He told himself he would make a terrible adventurer, blaming the shrapnel that had finally been dug out of his forearm only three years ago.

Indoors, he was on surer ground. His tutorials always started off as affable affairs, with Lewis lounging across his Chesterfield and scattering ash everywhere as he switched from pipe to cigarettes. It was a disarming sight. Yet, like his Irish solicitor father, he would pounce on any hint of sloppy thinking. And he always loved goading his students on to greater things.

The don sighed and shifted on the creaky sofa. 'Well, there's no use waiting for Miss Temple if she's mislaid her brolly. She's usually as regular as clockwork, as we know, but *The Faerie Queene* won't wait for her. Give me the benefit of your expertise on the virtue of chastity as embodied in the character of Spenser's warrior princess Britomart, Mr Henchard.'

Sometimes, Lewis found himself wishing that a latter-day

Britomart might rise up and fight on behalf of her fellow females. Although women were few and far between at the university itself, they had formed a majority in the city during the war with so many men having been conscripted: every tinpot London company, not to mention many of the hospitals, seemed to have moved its mostly female staff there because of the bombing.

As well as the city's opportunistic bootleggers, the Yanks at nearby RAF Bicester would lay siege to this abundance of hungry and lonely women with gifts of lipstick and nylons as well as edible treats or chewing gum. The reputation of Oxford's Randolph Hotel for all-night trysting had reached even the don's cloistered ears, with Lewis quickening his pace as if he might be corrupted every time he walked past it on a Tuesday lunchtime to meet John Tolkien and other chums over a pint at the Bird and Baby.

One of the regulars in the Eastgate, a rival establishment, used to swear that all through the war discarded condoms were thrown into the pile of rubbish at the back of the Randolph, a yarn that Lewis had to put firmly to the back of his mind whenever he was asked to give wartime theology talks at the nearby air bases. In his heart, however, he felt that he couldn't condemn. Besides, it was a world he knew nothing of, save for the occasional bit of gossip in pubs and a barmaid's sometimes knowing looks.

As for female students, 'too pretty' was his facetious blanket excuse if anyone in the Senior Common Room asked him over a glass of sherry what he thought of their presence. He knew it was just the interrogator's impudent way of being nosy about one of the university's more eligible bachelors, who surely must be in want of a wife to sort out his haphazard life or at least get the old fool a decent suit.

The Magdalen muckrakers had long been exasperated by the enigma of Lewis's domestic situation, under the thumb of an old lady at home according to the daily helps that she bullied. He had lived at The Kilns since 1930 with the mother and sister of his dead fellow officer and friend Paddy Moore, who had been killed in action towards the end of the First World War, while Jack, wounded by shrapnel from a shell, was invalided back to England.

Separated from her husband, Paddy's mother, Janie Moore, had developed a strange possessiveness towards Jack – at least in the opinion of others, including his brother Warnie – despite the 26-year age difference. At 18, he and Paddy had made a pledge that if either perished in the war, the survivor would take care of the dead man's parent. So Jack, Janie and her daughter Maureen shared a succession of Oxford lodgings until they and Warnie clubbed together to buy The Kilns for the four of them to live there. After Maureen had moved out, following her marriage in 1940, Janie – nicknamed Minto for the mints she liked to guzzle, though not for a sweet disposition – jealously guarded her position as the only resident woman in Jack's life.

There was certainly no sign of Lewis wanting to share with a bride the rumoured wealth that his bestselling books had brought him on both sides of the Atlantic. He seemed wedded to his work, and a casual fob-off to the curious would usually stop any further mention of the matter, especially as some of the other dons' wives seemed to share his view that women could be a distraction. Like

John Bunyan's Christian, he tried to avoid temptation, treating even barmaids as respectfully as novice nuns.

Suddenly, as Henchard tried in vain to give the impression he had even read *The Faerie Queene*, Lewis remembered the unusual thing about Susan Temple. For a number of tutorials now, she had not been wearing her figure-hugging suits, glimpsed beyond the open flaps of her black academic gown. She was usually quite the glamorous mannequin; sometimes he wondered how she pulled off such a trick, since Minto was always complaining about the impossibilities of fashion on the ration.

Yet, recently, Susan had taken to turning up to his rooms in a heavy coat that she never once removed, despite the fires that Squirrel made up in the grate. Lewis had also noticed that Temple seemed withdrawn, her face puffy and fatigued, with none of the almost insolent pertness that he rather admired.

After encountering her narcissistic mother the year before, when Temple had been driven up from London by her parents to join all the other freshmen for the formal introduction to their first term, he could quite understand the daughter's battle-ready behaviour. Her mother was an armour-plated siren, flaunting an ivory cigarette holder and flirting with everything in trousers while her dry old stick of a husband stood grimly aloof. She had stared lingeringly at the don, enjoying the evidence of her provocative effect in his dark eyes.

'Oh, Professor Lewis, I was so looking forward to meeting you and hearing about those wonderful books of yours,' she had purred, raising one perfectly etched eyebrow and scrutinising his shabby suit as if she doubted the old buffer's successful reputation as an author. 'You're quite the celebrity, I'm told, especially with the Yanks and all their dollars.'

He realised she had sought him out, dragging her husband and daughter over from Somerville. Seeing Susan's embarrassed scowl, he had ignored this conversational equivalent of a bank raid; it was none of her or any other tittle-tattler's business what he did with his royalties. If he had revealed that he privately gave most of it away, the woman would have been incredulous – and probably even more impertinent. Instead, he had replied mildly, 'Very kind, Mrs Temple, but I don't actually have a professorship; I'm just plain Mr Lewis to all my students.'

Smiling satirically, she had turned on her French heels and walked towards another group of dons as Mr Temple abruptly gripped Lewis's hand – a bone-crusher if ever there was one – and said goodbye.

Lewis had been curious about Susan's home circumstances ever since. He had been almost tempted to put an avuncular arm round her shoulders as she sat hunched up during their last essay-dissecting session and ask how she was, but of course that would never do.

'Never make the mistake of getting too close to the female students: even with the most honourable of intentions, it will always be misinterpreted.' With a jolt, he remembered the timely warning from his worldly friend Dorothy Sayers – an alumna of Somerville.

It was often admiringly said that Dorothy had covered the entire spectrum of human wickedness in her crime novels, which made her seem something of an oracle in college circles, where the everyday brutalities of the outside world rarely seemed to penetrate. All he knew of that was what he read, or what he wrote in his bestselling theology books and his science-fiction thrillers about the eternal battle between good and evil. After all, he was just a cloistered academic with a vivid imagination – and an abiding interest in human nature.

As his closest female chum, Dorothy was old enough and respectable enough – safely laden as she was with the baggage of her invalid husband Mac – to pass muster with all the gleaming-eyed gossips around him. And she always seemed to speed-read Lewis like a book. He wondered whether he should pass on to her his worries about his missing student.

Why the devil had Temple been feeling the cold so much? The question niggled away at him. What do I know? he concluded. I'm just a silly old bachelor. Young women and their wardrobes are a mystery, thank goodness, and long may it stay that way.

Bad idea to get involved. And yet . . .

He resolved to drop a few lines to Dorothy anyway.

CHAPTER 2

For the umpteenth time that morning, Lucy Standen had traipsed down to the basement to collect a book ordered by a teacher. She had been at Oxford University Press for nearly three years and was now seriously plotting her escape.

The basement was where the elementary-school boys shared a smoke and a snigger in between filling the vast racks with volumes from the trolleys. Hired for their muscle, they were given regulation brown overalls to differentiate them from the scholarship boys since they were considered factory hands, not clerks. During their dreary daily OUP routine, there was always the chance of enlivening things by leafing through what they thought of as a 'dirty' book, such as the much-thumbed medical one with sepia photographs of the genitalia of rare hermaphrodites.

One of the elementary-school boys, Eddie Jarvis, always seemed to be in Lucy's way somehow. Olive-coloured eyes, almost like army khaki. Wet lips. Hunched, bat-like shoulders and a long-armed reach with big hands. There was something hungrily avid about him. She would squeeze past his bony body with elaborate care as if trying to insinuate herself into a very narrow imaginary gap, rather like the rubber-bodied mime artist Monsieur Marcel Marceau in that performance for the troops that she had seen on the newsreels at the pictures during the war. Wary of any contact, she took care never to lock eyes with him.

The grammar-school boys, destined for the Dickensian heights of head clerkships, never hung around downstairs for long but shot back up to their desks, which were arranged in rows like a classroom with the supervisor's desk facing them. At nearly 19, she was older than many of them.

Institutional cream and olive-green paint made the offices drearier than they should have been, given that the honey-coloured building was considered by Oxford snobs to be a particularly handsome example of neoclassical architecture in the local Headington limestone. Yet at first sight, its many-paned windows gave it the look of a vast gaol. They were never opened either, so the airless atmosphere was pervaded by the sickly smell of floor polish that reminded Lucy of her old assembly hall.

What was the point, she thought, of having a job if it's just like being back at school?

Ignoring the sly, sideways glances that always came her way in the basement, she trudged upstairs again to enter the order in the Kalamazoo ledger in her neat italic hand.

She was the only girl there, addressed as 'Miss' by the supervisor who could never – would never – remember her name. The boys were all called by their surname with no dignifying 'Mister' before it; that came with seniority.

No one ever chatted upstairs, except occasionally and quietly round the tea urn. Lucy still missed her encounters with Charles Williams on those breaks; he was never an ignorer of intelligence in the lower ranks. His sudden death after an operation two years before had come as a tremendous shock. She had been amused and touched by the fact that Williams, a formidably clever OUP editor, still spoke with a slight Cockney accent, like her London-born father. Lucy's accent had long since been ironed out by her grammar school.

Sometimes she had attended his lectures, which were always packed, in the university's Divinity School, although she had a secret horror of being thought to number among the fawning female worshippers who behaved like such ninnies in his presence.

Charles Williams had been renowned as the only intellectual in Oxford without a degree, having been forced to leave University College London when family funds ran out, and also for his surprising attractiveness to women. The expressiveness of that long upper lip, more conducive to comedy than to beauty, had often made Lucy smile as he put his points across with a flourish.

To her, he had always been gentle and considerate, even asking her polite and friendly questions about the deadly dull clerking. She sometimes allowed herself to hope that he might have recognised a fellow kindred spirit, albeit one who was in the wrong job.

At one of his lectures, she had found herself sitting next to a well-built, rather red-faced fellow who arrived a few minutes late and then dumped his brolly and briefcase untidily on the floor.

When Williams's talk came to an end and all his female followers set up their usual frenzied clapping, she sensed a certain disdain at their reaction in the aquiline profile of the burly man next to her.

Even a sideways view had been enough identification for Lucy, who recognised him from the inky little image that accompanied reports in the *Oxford Mail* about the wartime broadcasts by the Magdalen don and author C.S. Lewis. She also remembered reading that he was known as Jack, having called himself that instead of his first name Clive ever since his beloved dog Jacksie had been run over by a horse-drawn carriage when Lewis was four years old.

The weather-beaten complexion made him look more like a farmer than a dry old academic. In his newspaper mugshot, the dark eyes had looked calm and the mouth well shaped and sensual. Still covertly staring at him, Lucy suddenly had a strange feeling that she had seen this slightly shambolic figure once before. It was a few years ago, during the war, when she was still at school. She racked her brains, trying to recall the circumstances.

Bending down to pick up his muddle on the floor, Lewis stood up and abruptly exited the den of femininity, perhaps aware of her stare. He must be bashful around women, she hazarded, unlike Mr Williams.

It could hardly be called an encounter, yet Lucy remained curious about him thereafter. She began to obsessively scour the local papers for any more mentions of the great man, sometimes scolding herself for behaving like one of that singer Frank Sinatra's hysterical bobby-soxer fans. The truth was that, despite herself, she had begun to fall in love with another world and the life of the mind.

She looked up at the large wall clock above the supervisor's head.

Ten minutes till lunch and then only time for a quick tea and bun in Joe Lyons on Cornmarket with Susan Temple, who had sent a note out of the blue saying she wanted to meet her there.

Why Susan didn't simply drop round to Lucy's house in Jericho was mystifying. After all, her father, Alfred, was always happy to put the kettle on, and Susan's discreet visits to what Lucy wryly thought of as their humble home had been fairly regular since she'd got to know the Standens.

Sometimes Lucy wondered whether her father was too gentle to be a scout. The brawny-armed college manservants were a famously tough breed, hauling buckets of coal up every staircase, placing bets on the sportier students, sometimes looking askance at the more scholarly types and uncomplainingly clearing up the marathon student drinking sessions of which they tacitly approved as a young blood's birthright.

There were rumoured to be some bullies among their fraternity, and Alfred would do anything for a quiet life, which usually meant he didn't get one. Whenever she got so frustrated with her father that she would talk about going into battle on his behalf, he would just smile and call her 'Lucy Lionheart'. But there was a limit to what she could do to protect him: college rules were college rules, and his refusal to shop Susan Temple last June for catching her in a male student's Christ Church rooms overnight had been a huge risk for him to take.

Susan's own father was a headmaster and a stickler for strictness, or so she implied whenever she called round to Alfred's place. Her aloof mask always slipped in his company; he seemed such a guileless man that people dropped their guard. Lucy was different, but after a chilly start, Susan seemed to have decided she was worth talking to. There was a year between them, but that didn't matter with a servant's daughter; age was the least of the barriers.

'Meet Lyons lunchtime Tuesday,' her note to Lucy said, with a haphazard S scrawled at the end. Susan had never summoned her in this abrupt way before. It was a terrible place to have a conversation; you could hardly hear yourself think amid all that clatter. Was that the point? Lucy couldn't work it out. And why was she allowing herself to jump through hoops for her, anyway? They had nothing in common; it was a friendship she couldn't explain. Yet there seemed an unspoken need in Susan for the plain home comforts of Alfred's little domain that his daughter found intriguing. And judging by the sprawling calligraphy, Lucy guessed the note had been written by a hand that couldn't stop shaking with nerves.

So, as the clock in the Oxford University Press struck, she unhooked her coat and beret from the peg rail and ran obediently out into the rain to do her friend's bidding, consumed with curiosity and unaware that someone was following her.

CHAPTER 3

'I'm Fetch,' the bulldog said to the youth, smiling slightly. 'It's what I do.'

The Bulldog in St Aldate's was a redbrick Victorian building with large windows, much frequented by the college policemen known as bulldogs who felt they owned the place because of its name. Sometimes they found themselves drinking alongside the odd intrusive copper from the official city police station across the road, hence a certain atmosphere that had led to the tavern's nickname of the O.K. Corral.

The pub was a regular drinking den for Mick Fetchley, known to friends and foes alike as Fetch. He had placed his back to the window in his usual spot, directly opposite a sulky-looking young man sitting on a bench. The light falling on the youth's face made it an illuminated picture against the brown-painted walls for anyone who cared to study it.

Fetch was a big man, aware of his imposing build. Women found him oddly attractive, probably because of the bright blue eyes in a pink-skinned face and the ostentatiously brilliantined dark hair. He didn't care about that: bints had their uses, but he always felt more comfortable in male company.

He missed the army: he had had a good war, especially in Egypt when the Tommies would bellow 'King Farouk, King Farouk, hang your bollocks on a hook' as the British soldiers marched captive Italian soldiers into Cairo. You felt like a bit of a king yourself at that point.

Yet he had made quite a bit of money since he got back to Oxford via London. Rationing was a mug's game, and there were always ways round it. His old bulldog job at Christ Church provided plenty of front for those with a sideline and had been obligingly kept open for him throughout the war by the proctors. When it came to policing the college, they preferred single men with no families to distract them, especially ones like Fetch with a bit of experience and enough wolfish cunning to root out the rule-breakers.

And the compact size of his little home city suited him. He couldn't wait to leave demob London after the Yard started up its post-war Ghost Squad, an undercover operation that was a bit too bloody good at sniffing out the stuff that had fallen off the back of a lorry. Too much competition from other gangs, as well. Then there were all the deserters still milling around in the Smoke, relying on the likes of Fetch to help them keep body and soul together. The main thing was to try to avoid the serious head-cases among them.

The rough stuff Fetch left to his small army of boys, whose youthful callousness could carve its way through anything. The plans to bring National Service conscription in next year for youngsters was bad news, true, but Fetch was already working on that with fake ID cards so the lads could claim Irish ancestry and disappear to the Republic for a while.

'Cig?' he said affably to the youngster on the bench, offering him an Abdulla.

'Don't mind if I do,' said the boy after a momentary hesitation. You weren't a man if you didn't smoke.

Olive gaze stared at blue, trying to assess.

'I'm Jarvis, Edmund Jarvis,' muttered the youth eventually. 'Most people call me Eddie.'

'So, what's your line, then?' said Fetch.

The young man told him where he worked and no more, reluctant to give too much away to someone who might be trying to flog him something dodgy. He had heard about such things.

'Oh, very impressive,' said Fetch sarcastically. 'I'm not a great one for book-learning myself. But the thing about people who've got their heads stuck in books is that they never notice the bleeding obvious.' He had been intrigued by the morose look on his new drinking companion's face; with the old codgers, you could understand it, but not with someone as wet behind the ears as this kid. 'What's up?' enquired Fetch conversationally. 'You look a bit down in the dumps. You need a plan to cheer you up, that's what.'

Everyone had to have a plan: you had to beat the system because it was always stacked against you, just like one of those fairground stalls where you could never win, no matter how good your aim, unless you worked out how they were diddling you. And then you had them.

Jarvis returned his stare and then mumbled, 'Thing is, there's this girl.'

'Oh, there's always a girl,' said Fetch indifferently. 'Fancy another pint?'

The boy's lips seemed to glisten at the offer of ale.

'You're new in town, aren't you?' said Fetch. 'Relax, you'll be okay.'

The youth bridled. 'I've been here since the London office moved here during the war. My family came too after we nearly got bombed out in Lewisham.' He added, 'I know I look old for my age' – although to the other man's eyes, he didn't – 'but I've only just turned 19, so maybe that's why you haven't seen me around.'

It was obvious that he was still finding his feet, but there was a sheen of resentment mixed with the naivety that Fetch thought might come in useful. As if to prove it, the boy added, 'Oxford still seems a bit cliquey if you ask me. And the bints are really snooty.'

'Is that so?' said Fetch, wrinkling his nose theatrically. Then he smiled again. 'Is there one in particular who's been bugging you? I know what's going on around here, and you'd be surprised. Be very careful, my lad. You don't want to get trapped.'

'What do you mean, "trapped"?' asked the boy suspiciously.

'In the way men always are,' said Fetch. 'If you ever get into trouble, let me know. They've got a place for 'em here. It's just down the road, but it's hidden away. Very discreet, they are. They know what to do with them all right. There's a very good system going on here.'

Jarvis leant forward awkwardly, still trying to read the expression in the bright blue eyes. Fetch looked at the boy's crumpled tweed jacket – poor quality schmutter by the bulldog's standards. I could get him a good double-breasted demob but he probably wouldn't know the difference, he thought. Aloud, he merely remarked, 'See, the thing is, you gotta be ahead of the game. Stick with me, kid.' The kid instinctively squared his bony shoulders, trying to be the big man.

Marcia leant across the bar, looking curiously at Fetch's latest quarry and showing off an impressively tethered top half as she rested it flirtatiously on the counter. 'Another drink, dearie?' she enquired of Jarvis, though she knew full well who would be paying. She had run these premises all through the war while most of the men were away, either fighting or dodging the fighting, and she knew how to rule her little world with the lightest of touches.

Fetch's intent stare slid round to her briefly. 'Yeah, we'll have two pints of stout, Marce. Don't rush. We're in no hurry. Nice and snug here.'

CHAPTER 4

Minto was giving Jack hell from the redoubt of her bed, roaring like a tiger cub when she had the strength and mewing like a petulant kitten when she did not.

He had sluiced the downstairs flagstones and run the carpet-sweeper awkwardly across each step of the stairs – Was there ever such a useless object? Better to beat the dust out instead with a hard bristle brush when he had the energy – but that insistent voice penetrated his labours every time. The ailing Minto, plagued by leg ulcers and beginning to show signs of senility at 75, was forever falling out with the maids, who kept handing in their notice – leaving Lewis to mop up the worst of the dirt.

In Warnie's opinion, his brother had fulfilled, many times over, his side of the sacred pact made with Paddy Moore. It was Paddy who drew the short straw in death, yet it was Jack who could be said to have drawn the short straw in life, as Minto's de facto servant forever after. She never spoke of her estranged husband, with Warnie suspecting she saw Jack as a substitute. Yet Jack always maintained that Minto was simply behaving like an overprotective mother who would regard any other woman as competition for her precious boy's affections.

The fact that the three of them owned The Kilns gave Minto the power of veto over who else could live there, and it was only too easy to imagine the comic horror of Jack trying to carry a bride over the threshold while that she-devil, as Warnie thought of her, guarded the entrance with bared fangs.

Her paranoid suspicions could certainly be a nightmare. She governed with a love that sometimes made Jack dread going home, but he accepted his yoke with what seemed to be the humble patience of a donkey. Yet he got a literary revenge in the end: Minto had no idea he had fictionalised his feelings in his book *The Screwtape Letters*.

Would his scout be surprised to find him on his knees with a scrubbing brush or helping Minto with her blessed marmalade-making whenever she had saved up enough sugar? His rooms in college were a paper-strewn pigsty, so perhaps it was divine justice that he should play the charlady at home.

He was hopelessly cack-handed, he knew, when it came to operating equipment, domestic or otherwise. For that reason, he had never learned to type or drive a car, even though he would have found both skills useful. Though his sense of duty had made him volunteer for the Home Guard during the recent war, he sometimes felt that a one-legged, wall-eyed poodle might have done a nimbler job. He knuckled down to all the dreary drill and the patrols in the early hours; however, reviving his rusty Great War skills at loading a rifle and then firing it at a target range of sacks with scribbly Hitler moustaches was quite another matter.

He had always found it hard to pull the trigger because of the deformity, shared with his brother Warnie, of having only one joint in his thumbs. As for bayonets, he fervently hoped he would never be expected to use one of those again – even on just a stuffed sack. There was something so *personal* about cold steel. From what he had heard, that lunge into another man's flesh could be felt all the way up the arm of the attacker.

He could just about handle a saw without doing himself a mischief, though Minto had expressly forbidden him to light a log fire in his study at The Kilns. Coal was still heavily rationed to 34 hundredweight a year, so it was a hard instruction. He had always been cheered by the homely sight and sound of wood spitting and crackling in the grate as he drew near to warm his mitts. The terrible arctic conditions endured earlier in the year still made his chilblains play up. Let's hope we're spared that again, he thought.

It had seemed like a frozen eternity, and any fool could have seen that it would be followed by floods and power cuts. Buses and even houses had disappeared in great drifts of snow, and when the heavens rained down upon them afterwards, both the Thames and the Cherwell burst their banks, the latter merging with the canal into one vast watercourse.

The countryside had it worse, of course: he had read somewhere that four and a half million sheep had perished before farmers could rescue them. There were times during that awful period when he felt almost surgically attached to his wellingtons, but

Minto, of course, never left her bed and her creature comforts, so she was blissfully unaware of his travails. Yet whenever he tiptoed up to her room, she would welcome him with a kiss to make up for being so crotchety, as she put it.

Her varicose ulcers were a dreadful trial, he knew, yet as he gazed at her dear face, he sometimes wondered to himself whether he would ever be quite free of her spell. He dared not mention this to Warnie, who often warned him not to play the martyr so much – ignoring the fact that Minto's domestic tyranny never stopped Lewis from producing books at his usual prodigious rate.

She had no objection to him beavering away in his study at home, from where at least he could be easily summoned. What she always wanted to know about were his movements beyond The Kilns. Although Jack's routine was as regular as clockwork, she was still suspicious, especially about his regular Tuesday meetings at the Bird and Baby with Tolkien and the other men in their writing group, the Inklings. It irked him that she often asked questions about the barmaids, as if he ever noticed who was serving him ale. Warnie had cynically suggested Minto couldn't believe how lucky she was to have such a loyal companion, which was why she never quite trusted him.

Rummaging through the landing cupboard, he realised it was time to get the flannelette jim-jams out. 'Good Lord, I'm a regular housekeeper,' he muttered, looking for a hot-water bottle and finding only a couple of ancient eiderdowns to replace the useless fancy candlewick bedspreads that Minto preferred but that never kept out the chill. His rugged old army blankets had been given to the Boy Scouts behind his back.

What's needed, he thought ironically, is a woman round here to sort us out. Maureen had been a great help in keeping her querulous mother in check when she was living with them, but since her marriage she hadn't visited nearly enough for Jack's liking. June Flewett, his favourite among the evacuee children who had been billeted at The Kilns during the war, still came up from London occasionally to stay and lend a hand, especially with feeding the hens, but they didn't see enough of her either.

Warnie was no help on the domestic front, interested only in the scandal of the potato ration brought in by the government that month. We would do better back in Ireland, reflected Jack, staring down at his stomach. At least it's a sacred vegetable over there. Warnie and he both had big corporations, and they needed filling up with proper fuel.

Food parcels from some of his more devoted American admirers still arrived, though less regularly than during the war. He was always scrupulous about sharing them out with Inkling friends over tea and tobacco with a jug of beer on the table in his Magdalen rooms on Thursday evenings.

What he and Warnie both sorely missed was a decent supply of sugar, most of the miserly rations having been commandeered during the war by the sweet-toothed Minto to make her rather watery preserves for the winter when she was still mobile enough. The brothers had made sure to stock the larder up with tins of Lyle's Golden Syrup, an old childhood treat that the food factories continued to churn out. They even stirred furtive spoonfuls into their tea sometimes.

As a boy, Jack had been fascinated by the tin's poignant image of a lion lying on the ground, a swarm of bees around his body, with a quotation from Samson's riddle in the Old Testament's Book of Judges: 'Out of the strong came forth sweetness.'

With all the factual brutality of a legal mind, his father had explained to the child that the insects were building a honeycomb inside the carcase of the beast. And yet there was something romantic about the drawing nevertheless.

Seeing how upset the boy was by the explanation, his mother had whispered in his ear that the fallen king of the jungle was not dead but only sleeping, the better to conserve his strength. Which was why the adult Jack often went to the Ashmolean in Beaumont Street to linger in front of an Egyptian pottery lion from the sixth dynasty, finding something appealing about the tranquil wisdom of the tiny creature's gaze.

He knew he was guilty of anthropomorphising, but was not the lion the patriotic symbol of England? He smiled as he remembered Susan Temple bringing up the Romantic poet Shelley when they were supposed to be discussing Medieval English. She had quoted 'Rise like lions after slumber / In unvanquishable number!' from Shelley's poem *The Masque of Anarchy*, claiming it was a great favourite among socialists. 'Not quite your style, Mr Lewis,' she had dared to tease him.

Perhaps what he called his constant state of peckishness was beginning to make him hallucinate about God's creatures in this way. He had noticed that, as the nights grew colder, foxes would gather at the edge of the woods near The Kilns. The icy patches made it harder for them to forage, of course, and he couldn't help feeling sorry for the poor creatures. But Minto wouldn't hear of him or the daily maids leaving out scraps for them; she claimed it would attract rats.

When he leant out of his bedroom window one night to look up at the full moon, he suddenly had a wild notion that the vulpine little silhouettes resembled a pack of wolves. He recalled Warnie, an avid picture-goer, describing a newsreel about Hitler's wolf pack, the Nazi SS. Tempting, Jack thought hazily, to imagine the four-legged kind slinking through the Oxfordshire frost and ice like a platoon of secret police, sniffing out their victims. It was all the fault of the recent conflict, those lurid totalitarian nightmares of his. He had then stumbled back to bed, where he fell asleep again and dreamt of the Lady Margaret Hall girl who had never woken up.

Trying to focus on practicalities, his mind switched back to his missing star student. With Oxford's short eight-week terms, the workload was intense, and it made no sense in any case for such a bluestocking to go AWOL from her tutorials.

You might as well expect a dog not to want a daily walk.

CHAPTER 5

A few months earlier, in June, Susan Temple had found out where Alfred Standen lived in order to make sure that he would keep the secret that could get her sent down from Oxford.

One early morning, at the beginning of his shift, the Christ Church scout had caught her in Olly Crombie's bedroom. The night before, they had been celebrating the end of English exams at a dance. Olly had been circling her for some while, murmuring about her Pre-Raphaelite looks and watching her catch her breath. To the sounds of the band playing the deliciously ungrammatical 'Is You Is or Is You Ain't (My Baby?)', she had finally, defiantly succumbed to the sexiness between them.

The Lodge gates were always locked at 11 p.m., and men and women were forbidden to stay overnight in each other's segregated colleges. But Alfred mutely allowed Susan to leave the way she had arrived the previous night after following Olly over a scalable bit of the college wall near the Meadow.

After a pretext to her own scout, Hilda, that a kind-looking man had rescued her when she slipped in a rain puddle outside Christ Church in St Aldate's one day, Susan had quickly tracked Alfred down.

Some of the more desirable houses on Jericho's outskirts were substantial three-storey villas with fancy Moorish archways over their porches which appealed to the pretensions of the city's increasingly prosperous bourgeoisie. Alfred and Lucy's terraced Nelson Street home on the southern side, however, was tiny and faced with a grudgingly cut-price version of the area's Flemish bond chequerboard brickwork, as if to discourage the working man from aiming above his architectural station in life.

Alfred's astonishment at the sight of Susan on his doorstep made her stammer at first, something she had not done since school.

'I hope you don't mind, but I just wanted to thank you so much for not telling on me. I can assure you that it will never happen again.'

His daughter, Lucy, was in the scullery, frying up leftovers for bubble and squeak. The tiny flagstoned room was cluttered with damp clothes and sheets hanging down from a ceiling-attached pulley. A small washing machine and an elderly mangle had some-how been squeezed next to the stove.

In her childhood, Lucy had often played Dare with her friends by sticking fingertips between the wooden rollers of the mangle as someone else turned the handle and then pulling them out just in time before they were crushed. Lucy was good at the game, even though it gave her the horrors.

A tin bath hung from a large hook inside the back door, ready for the ritual of the weekly immersion in front of the living-room fire with sheets carefully arrayed over wooden clothes horses to provide an impromptu screen. The Standens made do with quick cat-licks and an occasional all-over wash the rest of the week, though Lucy sometimes felt self-conscious enough in the stuffy atmosphere of the OUP to wonder if her feet smelled.

Lucy heard a murmuring in the living room above the background chatter of the wireless. Startled, she opened the door to find a dark-haired girl with a pale face, high cheekbones and crimson lips in conversation with her father.

'This is the young lady I mentioned,' said Alfred. 'She's very kindly come to thank me, but I'm sure she doesn't need to. Don't worry, miss; my daughter Lucy knows how to keep mum. Come and sit down with us and share a bite.'

Lucy gave a cursory smile that barely hid her vexation. Dad was such a pushover, poor thing, ever since Mum had gone. But Susan's thanks seemed sincere, and she was taking as big a risk in visiting them as Alfred had done by not reporting her. Although Lucy always tried to ignore the colleges' ridiculous, archaic rules, she knew that town never met gown under such informal circumstances.

Across the oilcloth that had been spread over the table, Lucy's observant stare unnerved Susan as she carefully removed her coat and the little fawn hat worn at a jaunty angle. No forelock-tugging here. I'm a scarlet woman in her eyes, of course, an absolute hussy, thought Susan. No wonder she feels she can look me over. Yet, as the wireless burbled on, Susan began to relax under the other girl's curious scrutiny of her.

39

She was used to being looked at, anyway, and the surroundings were oddly comforting. Even the tin tub she had glimpsed hanging from the back door when Lucy emerged from the scullery looked cosier, oddly enough, than the plumbed one she had to share with several other women on her staircase at Somerville. Asking if she could be excused before eating, she was politely directed outside to a clean but spartan privy on the end of the house and next to the coal shed, with a roll of toilet paper hanging from a loop of string.

As she slipped her feet under the table and accepted a plate of delicious bubble and squeak with bread and dripping, Susan wondered whether this was how the other half always lived. The tea leaves brewed under the cosy, and her chilly face pinked from the warmth of the fire.

'Your father tells me you work at the Oxford University Press,' she said, trying to keep any condescending suggestion of surprise out of her voice. There was a slight pause, but Lucy's calm nod persuaded her to risk a confidence. 'We're neighbours: I'm at Somerville, just across the road from the OUP. If I looked hard, I could probably see you toiling away at your desk. Maybe we should meet up sometime.'

There was a sense of a tentative alliance being offered rather than a friendship, rather like the gatherings of girls in the dance halls facing the crowd of men on the other side of the room as if they were opposing armies assessing each other's strengths.

Lucy stared across the table at Susan's unreadable dark eyes. 'Okay,' she said off-handedly. 'Don't mind if I do.'

And now, facing Susan across the table at Lyons teashop, Lucy couldn't quite believe what she was hearing. In all their encounters since they had first met four months ago, the older girl had revealed little about herself except that she had an older brother, a prep-school master called Peter. Yet now Susan was revealing a far bigger secret than the indiscretion of spending the night in a male student's rooms without getting caught.

Somehow, she didn't seem the type to make the kind of mistake that could ruin her life. At 18, Lucy sometimes imagined herself to be a woman of the world, though she wasn't really. Susan, however, maintained the air of being rather higher up the evolutionary chain than most people, untroubled by the problems that affected mere mortals.

She spoke quietly, unnecessarily so given the usual hubbub of Lyons. The waitresses lived up to their nickname of 'Nippies', rushing between the tables with their laden trays. An elderly gentleman pointed to his half-filled cup of tea that exposed a large rim of white china round the top and complained loudly to a waitress with garishly applied lipstick. 'That's almost a clergyman's collar at the top there! Fill it up properly, if you please.' The girl sniffed and took the cup back to the counter to pour out more before returning to serve it with a petulant flourish.

Most of the customers, however, were groups or pairs of women, hence the noise levels of high-pitched voices, with only the occasional male one. It was certainly well chosen for someone who didn't want to be overheard.

'What will you do?' Lucy asked.

Susan flicked a look at her, gazed challengingly round the room and jutted out her little pointed chin in a gesture of defiance. 'I'm going to have to disappear,' she said. 'I've got a plan, but I need you to keep mum. I'll let you know how I get on; I'll drop you a line.'

'Aren't you going to tell your parents?' asked Lucy, bewildered.

'Don't be such a goose,' was the brusque reply. 'Your father is nothing like mine. Don't worry; I have it all under control.

'The doctor was a help, actually. He recommended this place: it's a hostel for women like me. The funny thing is that no one seems to know about it, not college people anyway. I've never heard any talk, even from the wilder girls, which is odd. You would think it would have come out somehow . . . But of course I didn't dare ask the scouts, even the one on my staircase, Hilda, who doesn't gossip like some of them.

'It's called Rake Hall. You go down this narrow twisting alleyway that seems to lead nowhere, and then suddenly it's there in front of you. Tucked away. I've gone there to register, and I just need to collect my things from Somerville and go back to Rake after sending some sort of plausible excuse – glandular fever, say – for leave of absence to the principal and the bursar.'

Lucy couldn't help looking impressed at such quick thinking.

'I've come up with the wheeze of glandular fever because a girl in my first year had it – and just disappeared home,' explained Susan. 'She's back now, but of course she had to retake that year.

'I suppose they'll let my tutors know in due course that I'm on sick leave, although they're really slow about organising things in the Somerville office – staff shortages ever since the war,' she added with a shrug. 'Any sickness is supposed to be reported to the college nurse, but I'll just say that I've seen my family GP.

'At this hostel, they're going to give me something frightful called a visiting moral-welfare officer employed by the charity that runs the place. Doesn't that sound ghastly? The damn cheek of it. But they told me that I'm very fortunate because the moral wotsit will have my best interests at heart,' she added with a mirthless laugh.

Lucy felt a sudden pang of pity.

'Thing is,' continued Susan, 'I wanted to let someone know where I was. I mean, it's important to leave a little trail behind you when you disappear for a while, isn't it? Just to be on the safe side. It's what they say in the detective stories that my brother devours: you need to have a pal on the outside when you go undercover – otherwise you'll be completely isolated. And I thought I'd be able to trust you because we don't mix with the same sort of people. I knew you wouldn't peach on me.'

'Oh, Susan!' Lucy's fingers were twisting her beret in her lap under the napkin. She felt helpless in the face of such a circumstance and dared not ask about the man, especially with the older girl looking as baleful as her dark beauty allowed.

'Oh, have some more tea,' said Susan scornfully, pushing the pot towards her. 'Do drink up. I can't bear it when people get mushy – and I thought you'd be the last person in the world with the sob stuff. If I want that, I can go to the pictures. Do buck up, Lucy. I thought you were rather a tough old thing compared to your dad. He's an absolute sweetheart, but anyone can see he's a bit of a softie.'

The other girl stiffened. 'There's a reason for that,' she said.

Susan wasn't listening; perhaps she never would. The friendship between them seemed more improbable than ever. Perhaps, thought Lucy, she was just being used.

She couldn't help feeling a little sorry for Susan all the same and decided to change the subject. 'What about your friends? Your studies?'

'I haven't got any friends,' said Susan abruptly. 'Not among the other girls, anyway. They think I'm a haughty bitch, and they may be right. There's one who's not so bad, but she's such a reclusive little thing that it's difficult to get a conversation going.

'Most of the men are frightful – so many big drinkers. They're always tight, and they're terrible letches. I hate myself for joining them sometimes, and you should see the way some of the barmaids look at me as if I'm no better than I should be. And the pubs are always being raided by the bulldogs – they just love lecturing us girls about unladylike behaviour.'

She began obsessively crumbling the uneaten bun on her plate, with Lucy nervously watching those angry fingers.

'This is such a misogynistic place!' Susan declared, exasperated. 'They never let us forget we're a minority, but I take the attitude that we've had to be better than the men to get into Oxford anyway. Mainly I just put my head down and get on with my work.

'But I'll miss my Medieval English Literature tutor, Mr Lewis. Did you ever hear his broadcasts on the wireless during the war? I used to listen to them in the holidays because we weren't allowed radios at school. He's such an earthy old character: being famous doesn't seem to have turned his head. He's sold masses of books – and his lectures are absolutely *packed*.'

For the first time since the two of them had sat down, the older girl had a smile on her face.

'He always seems in a tearing hurry, pulling off his coat and scarf while he starts talking and then flinging them on again as he winds up; it's a bit like watching a spinning top in slow motion,' she said dreamily. 'I love how fast and fluent he is, though apparently some of the snobbier dons say it's because he's got the common touch.

'He teases me sometimes about what he calls my militant atheism and says he'll convert me sometime. His first name is Clive, and some undergrads nickname him St Clive because of his books on Christianity, although his friends all seem to know him as Jack.

'I think he might be secretly a bit scared of women, but we joust away in his tutorials, and it's all rather fun. And I discovered recently that he enjoys Jane Austen, so he can't be a complete woman-hater.'

In the short time Lucy had known her, Susan had never looked so animated.

'Actually, I sat next to your Mr Lewis once,' Lucy ventured shyly, 'in a lecture by one of my OUP editors, Charles Williams. The two of them were good pals when Mr Williams was alive, both members of a group called Ink-something-or-other – so I heard on the OUP grapevine. I recognised Mr Lewis from his picture in the newspapers. He was quite burly, like some old country bumpkin with this awful squashed hat that he dumped on the floor. He really ponged of tobacco, too. I thought Dad was bad enough, but he was worse.'

'That's him,' said Susan. 'They call their literary circle the Inklings, which sounds such a hoot. I would love to be a fly on the wall when they get together in Mr Lewis's rooms and let their hair down over a few beers. My English professor John Tolkien is one of the members, too. But what on earth were you at one of Charles Williams's lectures for?' she added. 'You're not one of his dotty female followers who think he's God's gift to maidenhood, are you?'

She was smiling slightly, if curiously, at Lucy, who realised that the other girl was beginning to relax in her company for the first time since their almost-friendship had begun.

'No fear,' said Lucy, returning the smile with her own funny little lopsided one that gave her a look of wry amusement.

'So what will you do afterwards?' she asked again.

'I don't know yet,' came the brittle reply. 'I haven't decided. We're supposed to start thinking about our job plans in our second year, but it's certainly put paid to that for a while. My folks are keen on me going in for the Civil Service exam after I graduate, but I couldn't bear all that stuffy nonsense of a desk job for life and waiting for your pension.

'Between you and me, I'm rather tempted by the Foreign Office; they sometimes make approaches to Oxford and Cambridge undergrads. Tap them on the shoulder,' she added archly. 'You know what I mean.'

A movie memory about spies stirred in Lucy as she began to sense some common ground at last with this strange girl. It would have been nice to go to the pictures with her sometime, but she supposed it would be months before her new acquaintance saw the outside world again.

As if reading her mind, Susan said, 'I can only stay there for three months; there's a limit, apparently, because of the shortage of beds. Then I'll have to move on to another hostel. You have to go to ground, of course, until it's all over. I'll have to tell my folks afterwards, and I'm dreading that, but, knowing them, they'll just be relieved I'm sorting it out myself. As long as it's not on their doorstep, God forbid, as if I were some housemaid they'd have to sack for getting in the family way.

'They didn't notice anything different about me during the long vac, but then they don't usually notice me much anyway – and of course I hadn't started to show at that stage.'

Ignoring the slight against the serving classes, Lucy persisted, 'But what about your studies?'

Susan shrugged. 'I'm going to have to defer till next year. I can't see any other way round it.' Looking meaningfully at Lucy, she said, 'I'm just going to have to sit it out.

'But don't worry: I'm not going to do anything drastic.'

Lucy had not a clue what she meant.

CHAPTER 6

Ethel was a gifted design engineer, though not with steel, iron or nickel – those were men's materials – but with fabrics. She only needed to see a picture of a frock or a gown once to be able to recreate it to perfection. Her geometric mind easily mapped the two-dimensional picture to fit a three-dimensional body, and she cut the fabric herself without recourse to a pattern. Then her nimble fingers magicked up her wondrous creations.

Back in the summer, the arrival of Christian Dior's New Look boosted her trade. She had even been given a hush-hush commission to run up a copy of Princess Elizabeth's silk dress after the forthcoming royal wedding; it was for an overseas customer via a go-between. Ethel had insisted the gown be made up in a different fabric out of respect; she was a royalist and not one to take liberties.

When she measured a client up for a fitting, Ethel could sometimes tell before the woman herself that she was expecting. It meant no more orders for a while. An alternative source of income had quickly dawned on the dressmaker. Everyone had something on the quiet, didn't they? Widows had to make their mite where they could. Otherwise you couldn't survive. She had always been good with her hands, and even had the right sharp instruments.

So if the woman was not protected by a wedding ring – or if she looked worn out already from a succession of childbirths – Ethel always thought it worth a whisper in the poor dear's ear. Might as well be hanged for a sheep as a lamb, she reasoned. Given all the shortages, she could have got fined even for acquiring cloth without coupons – never mind the rest. One woman she knew had been jailed because she couldn't pay the fine.

Girl undergrads from nearby Somerville with money to spare began to hear of her dressmaking service. One of them called round quite often and was most particular about the latest styles. She never asked questions about the source, nor did Ethel venture any explanation. Within a year, she had become her best customer. It helped, thought Ethel, that she had an excellent figure – and never quibbled about prices. What a waste to go in for all that learning – that would never hook a husband.

Although some of the Varsity men might be a good catch, she supposed. They certainly seemed to have the readies, judging by how they spent it in the local pubs drinking yards of ale before rushing on to the next one as they tried to keep one step ahead of the sheriff. Raids by the university bulldogs were always dreaded: undergrads weren't supposed to drink in town but to keep to college bars, and the bulldogs often blamed the landlords.

A few of Ethel's neighbours in Cardigan Street belonged to the breed. All that power was bound to go to their heads, she reflected. The bulldog with the electric-blue eyes, who lived directly opposite her, drove a Triumph Roadster with those flashy front bumpers; even Ethel realised it must have cost a pretty penny. She had glimpsed him driving it into the dingy workshop of the little corner garage up the road as she passed by. Not the kind of place that women went into as a rule. But in her detailed way, she noted that he left it parked there off-street for quite a while, as if to tuck it away from prying eyes.

As she reached for her shears, she heard the usual two knocks on the front door. When the Blue Radar, as her neighbour opposite was nicknamed locally, had first heard on the Jericho grapevine about her seamstress skills, he sent round a young henchman called Sid to ask if she would like a delivery. Although she didn't altogether care for the impertinence of the youth's crocodile smile, Ethel inclined her head, and he held up ten fingers to indicate the price. She nodded, and thus Ethel's contraband fabric business began.

The henchman was outside in an old army greatcoat that served as a mantle over the bolt of fabric he was carrying upright like a rifle, clamped to his side. Ethel passed over the shillings, and then the kid, with his strangely taunting, ear-to-ear grin, melted away as if suddenly sucked back into the semi-darkness by an invisible force.

Ethel bent to her labours again under the light of an old gas lamp. She loved her work. In truth, it was no labour, even though her eyesight was getting so bad she thought she might need new spectacles. Yet she missed nothing and prided herself on being awkward (or okkered, as she pronounced it) when crossed. You had to be tough to be a widow, she thought. She threaded the tricky spool on her trusty old Singer and recalled the look of horrified revulsion on her best customer's face at Ethel's purred suggestion of a quick solution to the 'trouble' the girl had got herself into. Silly little bitch. She won't be wearing those fancy French fashions for a while. Shame. Wonder where she is now?

CHAPTER 7

A few terraces away from the dressmaker's house, Lucy was also wondering what on earth had happened to her friend in Rake Hall.

Susan's first letter had arrived with surprising promptness, given their short acquaintance. No one was allowed out, she explained, so she got the scullery maid to post her letters for a small consideration. All hush-hush, of course, and Lucy was to expect another communication as soon as she could smuggle one out.

There was a telephone there, Susan added, but it was in the office, which the manager took care to lock whenever she left the room. One way or another, there were a lot of jingling keys on chains to be heard in Rake Hall.

Every morning Lucy looked out for the postman. They didn't get many letters, apart from the time when they had received several in the familiar jerky writing that Lucy despised and wouldn't read on principle, leaving Alfred to sigh over another demand for money from his long-lost wife.

The next note from Susan had asked if Lucy would come and see her, so she did. The visit went off surprisingly well. Lucy thought she knew her Oxford like the back of her hand, yet she had never before noticed the narrow winding lane hidden in plain sight opposite the gardens and meadows of Christ Church in St Aldate's. Little more than an alleyway, it zigzagged round, as Susan had described, until it came to an abrupt stop at a high gate with the name in iron lettering across the top.

The gate was unfastened, much to Lucy's relief – she had almost expected giant padlocks in the Gothic tradition. Beyond it was a Victorian house adorned with a fanciful-looking turret that had seen better days. A short flight of stone steps led up to the front door. All very unremarkable, or so it seemed.

'I shall go mad if I don't see anyone from the outside,' the letter-writer had declared dramatically, so Lucy braced herself and rang the doorbell.

Eventually it opened, and she found herself looking at a surprisingly comely face with a cool expression atop what looked like a nurse's uniform. Lucy had not expected glamour in such a place: the woman's glossy dark hair was even styled in a fashionably long Marcel wave.

'I'm Susan Temple's sister,' she said, stuttering slightly over her cover story. A last-minute instinct had made her wear her reading glasses with the round black frames that dominated her small face.

'Indeed,' said the vision. A half-moon smile with closed lips gradually materialised as if being carved by an invisible hand into the marble flesh.

Lucy stared, fascinated. The eerie image of the slow-blossoming smile of Lewis Carroll's Cheshire Cat popped into her mind.

'I am Miss Ashover, the matron here. I wasn't informed about your visit, but you might as well come in. No doubt Temple would like to see you. Please bear in mind, however, that there are strict rules here and that only close family is allowed. And definitely,' she added, 'no male callers. We are a very respectable institution.'

Lucy followed the sheer seamed stockings – American, she suspected – and a glamorous-looking pair of court shoes into a hall with a sparsely furnished front parlour to the right, where she was told to wait while Susan was fetched.

Miss Ashover left the parlour door ajar, so Lucy took her advantage. Across the corridor was an office whose half-open door revealed cluttered surroundings, including several large filing cabinets and a middle-aged woman with a corrugated-iron perm and owlish spectacles. She was frowning over paperwork and typing like a rather tired woodpecker. In between the clack-clack, the occasional muffled noise could be heard elsewhere in the house – and at one point a distant baby wail.

At the end of the small hall were double doors with half-windows through which could be glimpsed a large winding staircase – oak by the look of it. The end of the rail was being slowly, reluctantly, polished by a young woman in an overall with her hair swept up into a bulky turban. She was facing away from the doors as if hiding herself.

Lucy retreated back into the parlour. And then suddenly Susan was before her, wrapped up in a long worsted coat, gloves and boot-ees. Her eyes were gleaming with relief.

'So good to see you, sis,' she said for the benefit of Ashover, who had followed her and stood silently by. They were taken past the rail-polisher and her studiously bent head to the back door, which Ashover unlocked, before ushering the two girls firmly into a frozen garden and then shutting behind them.

Aware that sound carried in frost, Susan lowered her voice. 'It's better out here. There's nowhere to talk inside. We all have to sleep in the one dorm, and there's always someone around. I expect Ashover only let you in because she's nosy about why my sister is visiting me. Most of the girls' families never come near them in this place – it's too much of a scandal. So we have to be careful.'

Shivering, they walked among the trees and the small patches of grass with doleful-looking evergreen shrubs here and there. In one corner, there was a vegetable garden that Susan said was the reluctant responsibility of the cook, who was always 'creating' about the time it took her to tend it.

'But it's her duty,' said Susan. 'After all, Somerville dug up some of its lawns during the war and planted them with vegetables instead. Everyone has to do their bit. But she thinks she's above all that. I don't know why she considers herself so important since she's a terrible cook – they could get someone better any day from the dole queues. But she's very thick with Ashover, it seems.'

She stared up at the battleship-grey sky and then turned around sharply to scrutinise the house and its paned eyes. Her face was tired and pale, a little puffier from when Lucy last saw her in Lyons. Is that what happens to you? thought the other girl, slightly in awe of the next mysterious process in womanhood beyond puberty.

Scowling, Susan paced around restlessly. 'We all have to work anyway. We do all sorts of cleaning jobs. They treat us like skivvies, and there's a lot to polish – especially those bloody staircase rails. They expect us to earn our keep with all this charring.'

'What do you do for money?' asked Lucy naively.

Susan snorted. 'Nothing doing with Family Allowance – they only pay for a second child, the meanies. I've got some savings – just as well since he's too broke to give me anything.'

'Who?'

'The man, of course. He's a member of the Bullingdon, and he can't really afford it – their bar bills are astronomical.' Seeing Lucy's blank look, she added, 'It's a dining club for the raciest chaps; they get up to all sorts there.'

'Wouldn't he give you a bit to stop people finding out?' asked the younger girl, feeling very daring for suggesting it.

Susan looked scornful. 'It wouldn't damage his reputation anyway if they did. I would just be regarded as the harpy who tried to hook him, so it wouldn't do me any good.

'The food at the hostel is vile – even worse than in college. They bulk our meals out with the vegetables, which I suppose is better than nothing. God knows what kind of meat we're eating. But it's not as strict as some homes, apparently. A couple of girls said they'd heard the Catholic ones are the worst.'

But the problem, she explained, with Rake Hall was that the Moral Welfare Association that owned it gave the matron free rein and never seemed to interfere.

'My moral officer is an old trout called Harwood who just came round on my second day to give me a pep talk about adoption and then never showed her face again. She gets through a fair bit of Mother's Ruin with Ashover, apparently, which keeps her sweet.'

Lucy looked blank. 'Gin,' explained Susan. 'What a joke. Mother's Ruin could have been made for a place like this. Although none of us is allowed to get our hands on it, needless to say. There's an office manager called Elsie, who logs all our details on arrival. She doesn't seem such a bad old stick. But Ashover seems to have it in for me somehow. She looked me over very insolently when I arrived.'

She paused and then said, 'Maybe that's because I had to admit to being an undergrad. She must have been hoping to see me squirm with shame at ending up here. I knew I was going to have to hand over my ration books for the cook's shopping trips, and of course my name and address are in them.

'But I just held my head high, brazened it out and pretended that my college knew full well I was expecting and had agreed to let me repeat a year after I'd got the baby adopted. I told her that because they valued me as a student they were prepared to make allowances. If only!'

'But won't they check with your college?' asked Lucy tentatively.

'I just have to take that risk. If they do, they'll find out that Somerville thinks I left because of glandular fever. But there's no logical reason for Ashover to contact them anyway if she thinks they know where I am.' Susan shrugged, sounding more confident than she felt.

The only alternative would have been new identity and ration cards forged on the black market with the connivance, according to a wild student rumour, of a fixer among the bulldog fraternity. Susan shuddered at the thought of adding criminality to her woes and then finding herself in the clutches of some rogue buller for evermore.

'What are the other girls in the hostel like?'

'They're all right. Mostly my age or younger. There are one or two 16-year-olds. Some of them seem quite dim, to be honest; the poor things go around looking like bewildered sheep. It wasn't till I got here that I realised why no one in my circles knows about the place: it's because everyone seems to be from pretty modest back-grounds. Maybe that's why they're all so meek and mild.'

She paused and narrowed her eyes. 'There's one who seems much older than the rest: I think she's in her late thirties. She only found out she was expecting when her teeth started to become loose. She must have been on such a bad diet that I think the baby started to cannibalise her. Can you imagine?'

Lucy could.

'And there are some who seem quite paranoid. A couple of them kept telling me their babies had been taken away by the secret police. Perhaps that's what the adoption process feels like to them. They've probably been reading too many novels – or else it's some kind of post-partum depression.'

Seeing Lucy's fearful look, she explained: 'It's what some women can get after they give birth. I looked up some medical books in my college library before I came here.

'I suppose those girls latched on to me because I'm new here. The others must have heard it all before, so I get it instead. Elsie records all the adoptions, which presumably they agreed to, so I don't know why they're getting in such a state. Maybe the poor kids regret it afterwards.

'But there are a couple of rebels here – and I intend to join them,' she added, the light of battle in her eyes.

'How?' asked Lucy, intrigued, but her friend smiled enigmatically.

'It's not known as "the home for naughty girls" for nothing,' was all she would say.

They paced around the garden for another five minutes until the numbness in their faces became too much. Susan sighed, making for the back door again. Just before they reached it, she inclined her graceful neck towards Lucy, who was shorter, and whispered, 'Some of the girls cry and cry for days on end after their babies are taken away.'

CHAPTER 8

The ash blonde was colloquially known as Cyn, short for Cynthia Carter. When Susan first arrived at Rake Hall and was shown by Ashover to her allocated dormitory bed and side table, Cyn had given her a meaningful look from the next bed, where she seemed to be engaged in an elaborate task of shoe-polishing.

'Move yourself, Carter,' said the matron. 'You're due for laundry duty.'

The blonde followed Ashover out of the room with a certain swagger to her hips, smiling satirically at Susan as she went. She seemed older than Susan, maybe about 21, but perhaps that was simply her worldly air.

At first glance, the long, high-windowed dorm had looked like any other. Having been to boarding school, Susan was familiar with all kinds of dreary institutional privations, especially the filthy food served up almost as a matter of principle in order to improve the backbone. Noticing the skeins of fluff draped like curtain swags where the walls met the ceiling, she concluded that cleanliness was obviously not a priority either. Waking up in there felt a bit like living in Miss Havisham's spectral mansion.

What she had not foreseen was that adult civilian women were expected to sleep communally with no privacy, not even a curtain between the beds as in a hospital. She had also vaguely assumed that there would be a cot beside each bed, but no: the place looked as spartan as an army barracks with its grey blankets and lumpy-looking pillows.

Where do they keep the kiddies? she thought.

The only other person now in the room was a meek-looking woman with short, sparse hair who smiled shyly at her. Judging by her even sparser teeth, she was probably about 40. A lot of people had dentures by then. Susan sat on the bed next to her and forced herself to smile back, introducing herself. The other woman, Bertha, was beginning to show.

'When are you due?' asked Susan.

'In about five months,' said Bertha, wincing.

Susan suspected it might be her first: she looked so lost and vulnerable. 'Where are the babies?' she asked.

'Upstairs in the nursery. You're only allowed to see them during the day. That's when you learn how to breastfeed, apparently. Overnight there's a visiting night nurse to give them the bottle. Probably better that way or none of us would get any sleep.' She smiled weakly, obviously trying to make the best of it.

There was a wedding ring on her finger. 'What about your

husband?' Susan asked, amazed to find a married woman in this place among all the unwed so-called sinners.

Silence . . . and then the floodgates creaked open as they sometimes do if the lonely mistake curiosity for kindness.

'He wasn't the father. I was married before I met him, but it had to be annulled because it couldn't be consummated. My family were strict Baptists and ever so upset at the annulment. They were really worried about the neighbours knowing. I had to give evidence here in Oxford in a closed court. It was awful. But then I met the other one.'

'Who?'

'He worked behind a bar and sometimes in a garage. He was Irish. I must say, the Catholics know how to enjoy themselves.' A faraway look appeared on her neat little features. If she weren't so sunken-cheeked, thought Susan, she could almost be pretty. 'They like a drink, they do. Not like the Baptists.'

Only a glass of champagne . . . she lost her good name, all through a glass of champagne. Susan thought of the music-hall song, often warbled by her tank-like old nanny – fortified by a secret slug of whisky in the nursery after Susan's mother had wafted in to say goodnight before going out for the evening in all her gossamer gorgeousness.

Too beautiful, really, to be a headmaster's wife, though not too beautiful for all the cocktail parties she went to without him. Not until she reached her teens did Susan fully realise the reason for so much iciness at home.

Her dormitory companion seemed keener on remembering the drink rather than the man – though if she had signed the teetotal pledge as a Baptist, that was only too understandable. Hoping she was in the presence of a new friend, she timidly confided that she had thought she couldn't get pregnant. 'You know, because of the non-consummation – I thought I wasn't like other women.'

Even Susan, not one to ladle out the sympathy, was forced to concede that the poor old dear couldn't have stood a chance against the wicked wiles of men. After her divorce, she was probably desperate for affection.

But then I'm a fine one to talk, she scolded herself.

'I didn't realise I was expecting until my teeth became loose. My doctor said it was because the baby needed nutrients.'

'What did the man say when you told him?' asked Susan, curious despite herself. Bertha trembled, her reedy voice suddenly husky. 'All he said was, "I bet you wish you'd never met me." And then a couple of days later, when I went round to the garage where he worked, they told me he'd got a girl into trouble and had gone back to Ireland.'

Susan realised that the men at the garage must have immediately guessed this immature middle-aged woman was the 'girl' in question when she turned up asking for him, looking distraught. How they must have sniggered behind her back. Men can be so horrid sometimes, she thought.

'I couldn't tell my family. They would have been ever so upset and angry – and anyway they're in London. And they wouldn't have me back there for all the neighbours to see. I wrote to a friend of mine, telling her that I was expecting and that the man had abandoned me, but she couldn't help me either. She lived with her widowed mother, who wouldn't hear of me moving in with them.

There was nowhere else safe to go, so my GP sent me here. At least we're hidden here.'

What a pitiful letter that must have been for her friend to read, thought Susan. Aloud, she demanded, 'Why should we hide ourselves away?'

The other woman simpered. 'You sound like some of the other girls here. They say that there are worse things you can do than have a child.'

At the sound of a sudden creak somewhere in the old building, she looked alarmed and dropped her voice to a whisper. 'Some of them are in such a state that they think their babies have been kidnapped.'

'Who?' asked Susan.

The child-woman looked down at the lino, saying no more.

Susan, who had been sitting with her back to the door, suddenly realised that the matron had materialised by her side.

'What were you saying, Temple?' said Ashover.

'Nothing, miss,' replied Susan, avoiding her eyes. Best not to get too bolshie too soon.

'Well, don't go upsetting Johnson here. She's fragile. Aren't you, Johnson?' Ashover took the woman's wrist and pinched the skin with her fingernails, lightly at first and then more deeply.

Then she looked at the new inmate again, unfurling her red-lipped smile. Despite the matron's calm demeanour, Susan sensed an aggression coiled within her. 'You're not due for quite a few months yet, so I think it's time you helped out in the laundry. Carter will show you the ropes. We do require girls to do their share of keeping the floors clean as well, though only for an hour or so if they're very far gone. It's important that we all pull together in our little community so that everyone knows the Christian value of good, honest work.

'I don't know if you've ever done any domestic work before. I imagine not,' she added, examining Susan critically until the young woman squirmed under the weight of her supposed privilege. 'But I should make it clear that we never risk the baby's well-being; that is paramount. You are a receptacle for a precious cargo, so you will be treated carefully while you are carrying it, make no mistake about that. I won't have anyone say that we don't look after the mothers who bear these unfortunate infants. We take all precautions. So, I'm going to take you upstairs first to show you how we do things here.'

A tentative, gap-toothed smile from Bertha conveyed a wordless goodbye to Susan, who followed Ashover up a narrow back staircase.

The stairs led to a birthing chamber where, explained Ashover, a doctor would be summoned if the midwives on call needed help with a complicated case. 'Nothing neglectful here,' she said. Next door was the nursery with a row of cots in which tiny whimpering infants in various states of wakefulness lay, presided over by a visiting maternity nurse who was showing several young mothers with babies in their arms how to guide them to the breast.

No one looked up as Ashover and Susan entered. Shoulders were defensively hunched as the mothers crouched over their task, shielding themselves from the world. In a glance, Susan priced their shabby home-made clothes to the nearest shilling. She had heard stories about some hostels, usually the most religious ones, where everyone had to wear hideous work overalls all the time like domestics.

How many women were in this place? Apart from Ashover, the cook and the scullery maid as the only live-in staff, she had been told that day nurses dropped in regularly to monitor the progress of the mothers-to-be. She was about to risk a question when Ashover abruptly told her to follow her downstairs to the basement laundry, where the lipsticked Cynthia Carter was waiting for them with hands on hips, ready to put the new girl through her paces. Her brazenness in front of the matron amazed Susan.

'Call me Cyn,' she smirked at the new inmate. 'I know everything there is to know about the laundry. Nappies, knickers, the lot. Splishee-splashee, as they say in the pantomimes.'

'Well, get a move on then,' said Ashover, smiling grimly at the witticism before resuming her usual aloof expression as she made for the door. That was the point when Susan realised that if you wanted to survive in this 'house of shame', you had to be utterly fearless – shameless, even.

Perching herself on top of an overwrought washing machine nearing the end of its cycle, Cyn swung her legs back and forth to show off a sleek pair of covetable nylons. Though her belly showed her to be about six months gone, her pins were still slim.

With all the noise in the background, it was the perfect time to talk privately. Susan looked down at her own still-shapely legs, wondering if they would hold up well; her mother had once told her about varicose veins and other abominations that came with having babies.

Now she found herself wondering whether that had been a veiled attempt to warn her off boys – or just another example of her mother's obsession with preserving a perfect beauty. God forbid that a child should ruin it. As the second-born, Susan was always made to feel that somehow she had compounded the damage.

'So, who got you up the spout, then?'

'Some married man,' lied Susan, wondering if Cyn and the other women had been told that an Oxford college girl was in their midst.

'Aren't they all. And they expect you to know what's what and organise it all. In my case, the damn Dutch cap didn't work. And my chap thinks all hell will break loose when this particular kid shows its face.'

'Why?' asked Susan.

'Because it will be a sweet little dark-skinned one, darling, with big brown eyes. They always look a bit cuter than white babies, don't you think? So Gawd knows why people are prejudiced,' said Cyn with a smirk as she fished a cigarette and a box of matches out of a pocket and lit up, sending a smoke signal towards the ceiling. 'I miss the GIs,' she reminisced. 'I think that's why I like the darker fellas – they're more exciting, more fun, just like the GIs. All those dances at the Randolph!

'I went out with an African-American GI for a while, and my Gawd, it caused a ruckus sometimes. Men glaring at us in the street, though never women, funnily enough. Some of them probably envied me. He was great at doing the jitterbug, though all the Yanks seemed to be pretty good at that.

'He told me the black men were treated really badly by the bigwigs in their military, but I don't see why – they were risking their lives like all the other boys, so why have it in for them?

'My boyfriend's from Jamaica. He's worried about my old man finding out about us and cutting up rough about the race thing with the baby, so I said I'd come in here and put it up for adoption. Well, that was the plan, anyway – but it's not the only option,' she said with an ambivalent grin before changing the subject. 'When are you due?'

'Late March.'

'Well, you'll probably have moved on to another hostel by Christmas then. There won't be any celebrations here, you can bet, though Ashover might hold a service to make us go down on our housemaids' knees again. She likes that.'

'Miss Harwood told me that we have to go to another one after three months because there are only so many places available – that's why there has to be a quick turnover,' said Susan, trying to string things out.

Cyn smiled. 'Too many girls ending up in the pudding club. And the men never take responsibility. A word of warning, dear: make sure you go to some halfway decent place for your last three months, maybe near your family – if they're still speaking to you, that is. This place is bad enough, but there are lots worse. I've got friends who can tell you some awful tales.

'Mind you,' she added, staring up at her smoke rings, 'there are always ways round it . . . if you put your mind to it. You could even stay here longer than three months if you sweet-talk Ashover enough; it might be worth your while.'

A baffled Susan stayed silent, hoping that Cyn's boldness might yield more. She didn't seem to be hinting at the very worst option for women in their condition, the one that made Susan shudder as she recalled the horrible overtures from Ethel during her last dress-fitting. The rumours around it always seemed to involve a lot of blood.

The other girl looked her over, visibly pricing her clothes. 'Nice bit of schmutter you've got there. Mind telling me where you got it?'

'A little dressmaker I know.'

'Oh, one of those! Be a pal and give me her address. You must have quite a bit put by to afford all that. Very few girls like that in here, I can tell you. Most of the posh lot get packed off somewhere abroad by their parents, so I've heard.'

Some survival instinct told Susan to play the long game and drop the cloak of arrogance in favour of the homespun smock of false modesty. Ashover already seemed to dislike her; she could sense it every time the matron looked at her. Susan remembered Peter once advising her, in his bossy elder-brother way, to choose her enemies carefully.

'I'm not well off. She doesn't charge a fortune.'

'Well, do tell,' urged Cyn, grinning with the assurance of one who knew she would get it out of her in the end. She had small, even white teeth, the bottom set slightly discoloured in the middle by tobacco, and exotic upward flicks of black liner at the outer edge of her eyes.

There seemed no harm in telling her where Ethel lived. And it was difficult to resist Cyn's persistence. Susan had always regarded herself as armoured in steel like an iron maiden, but then she had never really mixed with an outlaw with nothing to lose – least of all a reputation she probably never had in the first place.

Cyn showed no interest in delving into Susan's history, which was a blessing. Strange, however, that Ashover had not broadcast the fact that a snooty college girl had landed up in the same boat as the rest of them. Just the sort of thing that the matron might have crowed about, surely? Somehow the omission only added to the pervasive air of secrecy about the place.

Her thoughts turned to her brother Peter and the awful-sounding prep school he had gone to as a junior master after Cambridge. She wondered whether she should try to get a note to him via the scullery maid Vera to explain what had happened to her, just in case she needed another ally on the outside besides Lucy. Though he could be stuffy and dogmatic, Peter had a conscience. How he would react to her plight, she couldn't imagine; yet she couldn't afford to rule him out as a possible ally.

She realised he needed to be told her tutor Mr Lewis and her Somerville scout Hilda could be trusted as well as Lucy. When she had packed up her trunk to leave for the hostel, she pretended to Hilda that she had been diagnosed with glandular fever and would let the college office know she was going home to her parents. So diplomatic was the scout that Susan never knew whether she believed her. But she helped Susan to carry her luggage out to a waiting cab all the same.

Outside, snow was steadily falling; inside, the laundry room was a humid haven with its ironing boards and heavy irons and its overhead pulley maids laden with various hickey undergarments that made Susan feel itchy just by looking at them. One item was an enormous pair of bloomers made from parachute silk. I wouldn't be seen dead in any of that lot, she thought; I would rather go naked.

Her favourite choice of lingerie was delicate French knickers with a seam going all the way up the middle of the crotch, a garment notorious for making its wearer feel sexy. In her experience, the 'good' girls would always avoid them, going instead for the aptly named austerity knickers known as 'passion-killers'.

As the washing machine started shuddering to a theatrical close, the other girl stabbed out her cigarette into an empty rouge tin kept in what was beginning to look like a bottomless pocket, slipped down from her perch and moved closer, smiling sweetly with her finger on her lips just before the door opened.

Was she friend or foe? In this place, Susan had the feeling that there was no easy answer.

CHAPTER 9

The voice at the other end of the line sounded uncharacteristically wary for someone as fearless as Dorothy Sayers.

They had been friends and regular correspondents for several years, ever since forming a mutual admiration society over her radio play *The Man Born to Be King* and his satirical novel *The Screwtape Letters*.

After receiving Lewis's cryptic letter about what he had briefly referred to as a 'female pupil problem', she had rung him up. 'Tread very carefully in this particular area, Jack,' she cautioned.

'Well, of course I'm not going to blunder in. You can trust me for that. But knowing what a wise old thing you are, I just wanted to ask your advice.'

Lavish though they were with the contents of their wine cellars, Oxford college budgets did not stretch to the extravagance of installing exclusive single-line telephones for Fellows in their rooms.

To avoid anyone hearing more of their conversation on Lewis's shared party line, Dorothy suggested they have a drink together after a Monday-night Socratic Club meeting. It was one of the few events that brought her regularly back to Oxford, where she would stay overnight in a Somerville guest room while her husband Mac was being looked after by an agency nurse back at their Essex home.

As usual, they sought out a nook by the fireplace in the Senior Common Room, whose wood-panelled walls and ceiling provided the perfect sound absorption for a private chat in public. Armed with a whisky each, they lit up their cigarettes in unison, inhaled and leant back in their armchairs.

'Now, what's all this about, Jack?'

'One of my pupils seems to have gone missing, and I don't like it at all. I've had no note of excuse – nothing – and it's not like her. She's the best of the lot, a very able student. There's something odd about the whole thing, but I don't want to worry Somerville at this stage in case it rebounds on the girl. I just need to find out more facts first.

'I can't help thinking of that nasty case last term of the girl found dead in her bed in Lady Margaret Hall. The family testified she had had a bad heart since childhood, but there are plenty of tittle-tattlers saying that drugs may have been involved, even though no trace was found in her body. But it was just before exams, and she would have been up cramming half the night, so perhaps the poor girl felt she needed something to keep her awake.'

'Somerville had quite a rebel reputation in my day,' parried Dorothy, 'though perhaps that was just me and my friends. Do you think your missing pupil is the type to take drugs?'

'To be honest, no,' he said after a pause, 'not that I know anything about illegal stimulants or narcotics. But I think it would be a point of honour with her to get through exams without chemical assistance. However, my instinct tells me she takes risks in other ways.'

She leant towards him, lowering her voice. Even wooden walls had ears. 'So, how was she when you last saw her? What did she look like? Was there any sign of ill health or being under the influence of something? The problem is that girls know how to slap on the lipstick and powder in order to disguise something that you might spot more obviously in the men. They can be slippery little devils.'

Frowning, Lewis described Temple's appearance in her last tutorial.

Reaching for another cigarette from her red Sarony tin, Dorothy masked her immediate thought behind a comforting smile. 'I wouldn't worry too much, my dear – it sounds as if she's been taken unwell. Somerville will sort it out. Or her parents. You'll hear eventually.'

'But she doesn't like her parents. I detected a distinct atmosphere of hostility there, at least towards the mother, when I met them during Fresher's Week last year.'

Dorothy raised an eyebrow. 'I also think you're getting just a little too close to things here, Jack. This is a woman student – it's a delicate situation. For your own protection, you really shouldn't be asking too many questions about her. Especially as a bachelor without a wife by your side. Unmarried men can be quite vulnerable in these circumstances, you know. Fingers will point.'

Belatedly, it dawned on him that some might even wonder if

he was the blackguard responsible for his pupil's disappearance, trying to cover up his villainy by pretending to show concern for her welfare. Would he be suspected of molesting the girl to the point of scaring her away?

'These are deep waters, Jack, so don't get carried away,' she said gently. 'Let's have another drink before I have an early night. I think you need one, too, my old friend.'

CHAPTER 10

Despite Ashover's stand-offish, queenly air, Susan was puzzled to see girls seeking out the matron in corridors and in the front office, with the door closed firmly for quiet confabs. Some looked as submissive as supplicants, almost as if they were pleading with the odious woman in some way.

Adoptions, she supposed, must be quite a bureaucratic business, even though the system was brutally simple. You gave up the inconvenient baby to a suitable unknown couple and never saw it again. And that was that.

You were considered fortunate to be rid of the shame, the trade-off being that you were never allowed to know what had happened to the kid for the rest of your life. And neither was that child permitted any access to its original birth certificate to find out who its mother was. She tried to reassure herself that it was probably for the best.

The following week, Susan went down to the basement hothouse, not suspecting that it was to be her last time. A bell had rung earlier for the twice-daily group prayers in which everyone was expected to run, or waddle, to the refectory and sink to their knees or sit on a chair if kneeling had become a physical impossibility.

At the top table, Ashover, and sometimes Elsie, would drone through a few prayers to keep faith, presumably, with the respectable pretensions of the place. Susan had heard from one inmate that some very strict mother-and-baby homes marched their charges to church on Sundays in crocodiles like children, where they were expected to sit at the back so as not to pollute the rest of the congregation.

Ghastly cheek, thought Susan.

But Ashover didn't go as far as that, added the sly informant, because she didn't seem to want to draw too much outside attention to the place.

At the end of prayers, Bertha Johnson looked over shyly at Susan and kept close to her as they filed out for the daily household chores.

'I'm due in the laundry,' whispered Susan. 'Want to join me for a bit? We can have a chat.'

'I'm supposed to be doing the polishing,' the older woman muttered, 'but I might be able to sneak down there behind Ashover's back. Sometimes I even nip down to the kitchen to have a chat with Vera when Brumley's not around, 'cos we're not allowed there usually.'

That, Susan had discovered, was one of the surprises of the place. Even someone as meek as Bertha seemed to have her share of pert moments, rather like a sheep that baaed back at you.

Cyn had also taken a shine to Susan – or at least an interest. The blonde often seemed to be looking over at the newcomer, whether in the dormitory or in the refectory for mealtimes or at Ashover's prayer sessions. She always seemed to be in charge as the matron's trusty every time Susan was sent downstairs to do her dreary duty.

An instrument of torture awaited new inmates there: the vast mangle that nipped unwary fingers if they got too close while feeding sheets and clothes through its rollers. Susan, who hated machines anyway, struggled to turn the heavy handle, reluctant to show any weakness in front of Cyn.

The conversation started with the ways and means of obtaining hair dye, on which the bleach queen was an obvious expert, but when the washing machines started wailing and shaking like a row of shimmying showgirls, Cyn moved in smoothly for the kill. Her manner was solicitous but her eye was assessing.

'Have you made your mind up yet about what you're going to do?'

Feeling ambushed, Susan backed against the wall. 'I don't know what you're talking about.'

'Oh, come on, dearie. Don't pretend to be an innocent. You must have noticed a few things. Don't tell me you haven't seen some of the girls having pow-wows with Ashover.'

Susan tried, and failed, to look dim, years of private education having given her a certain front. 'I don't understand what you're on about,' she said stiffly.

'Well, you need to, pretty sharpish.'

The blonde lit another cigarette and took a long drag, flicking the ash on the floor for someone else to sweep up. 'You strike me as being quick on the uptake, so get your brain into gear for this one. There's a lot going on here. Ashover gives some of the babies up for proper adoption on the books to make everything look legit, and then she sells the others on the quiet.

'If you move fast, you might even get a bit out of it yourself. Most of the kids are going to be adopted anyway, so where's the harm?

'But you have to be tough with Ashover, or she'll go and do it anyway behind your back. Just make sure she knows you're on to the racket and want to do a deal with her. You have to play her like a violin. But be careful: if she thinks you're a threat in any way, you're for it.'

Susan began to stutter, something she had not done for years. 'B-but how can she get away with it? I mean, isn't it illegal to sell babies? Doesn't anyone go to the police?'

Cyn looked impatient. 'Why would they? Can you imagine most of the girls here having the gumption to go along to the station up the road and weep all over the desk sergeant? Who would believe them anyway? Even if it was properly adopted and all legit, they'd never be allowed to see it again anyway or know who adopted it, so what's the difference? Only the money that's made out of it in some cases.

'And Ashover would just deny everything if the mothers didn't have any proof. They wouldn't have been given anything to sign like they do with the proper adoption procedures, so they've got nothing in writing. She'd just say they're getting all emotional because of having to give up their babies to posh couples who'll give the kids a better life than a woman on her own could.

'I've seen a few of them try to argue with her, but they give up in the end. It's difficult to hang on to your baby even if you want to, so most just take the money and give in. Especially if it's the second or third time they've ended up in the pudding club. That's why she's not too fussy about a girl's background – unlike some other places.'

She looked sharply at Susan. 'Don't think it's easy to screw a good deal out of Ash. She's not that generous, and she keeps most of it. Although if you've got anything on her, you're laughing. She thinks I'm the entertainment round here, and she likes that, but in three months' time, when it comes to my turn to get my payout, I'm not going to be joking, I can tell you. I've got it all worked out. I might as well sell the kid – what have I got to lose?'

A vague memory of lurid newspaper headlines surfaced in Susan's mind – melodramatic stories of infants being handed over for cash at railway stations and given away through coded newspaper adverts, their eventual fates unrecorded and unknown and uncared about.

Raising her voice to make herself heard over the background noise, she said, 'Didn't they put a stop to baby-trafficking? Some Adoption Act or other during the war? I mean, you could get put away for selling babies. I thought that everything now was all done legitimately through adoption societies or local councils.'

Cyn looked across at her indulgently. 'They can try . . . but you can always cook the books. It's supply and demand, my darling. And since a lot of adoptions are private arrangements anyway, that makes it a damn sight easier for the dodgy ones to slip through.

'Sometimes Ashover lets the girls in the early stages stay on longer than the usual three-month rule till they reach their due date so that they can give birth here. If they're nice to her, that is.'

Susan realised she was talking to a recruiting sergeant.

'But what about the ones who don't want to give their babies up?' she stammered, feeling weak and foolish for saying so. 'There must be some who feel like that.'

Cyn looked mockingly at her. 'As I said, darling, they don't have much choice, do they? The government's not going to pay for it. I don't know anyone who can afford to keep her baby unless she can persuade the man to marry her and make her respectable, unless she's got a rich daddy who can hush things up and hire a nanny to bring the kid up somewhere quiet.

'Your type probably hasn't got a clue about most women's wages. No fun managing on a pittance and trying to keep your kid in a nursery at the same time.

'There's one idiot here who says she's planning to be a Ten Pound Pom and hop on a boat to Australia with her baby. Good luck to her, but she'll have to find a man out there to look after the two of them, same as she would here. I know there's a shortage of women over there and a lot of bachelor sheep-farmers, or so they say, but it's a hell of a long way to go to meet Mr Right.

'Her friend also wants to keep her baby, probably because she's older than the rest of us. Last chance she's probably got to have a kid.'

Her snicker made Susan wince for poor Bertha.

'But she'll have to hang on to it from the moment it's born – believe me, Ashover knows how to whisk them away. No way round it, most girls end up knuckling under and giving in to her. But at least the chosen ones get a bit of pocket money out of it.'

She put her head on one side like an inquisitive parrot, staring at Susan. 'What religion are you by the way, darling?'

'I was born a Catholic, though I don't bother going to Mass or anything now,' replied Susan, mystified.

It seemed to be the right answer because a broad smile spread across Cyn's face. As the washing machine she was perched on began shuddering to a close, she leant forward. 'You just have to know how to play Ash. She likes being treated like a queen. Between you and me, darling, I think you need to butter her up a bit more. She seems suspicious of you, and you've only been here five minutes, so what have you done to upset her?'

'Must have been the way I looked at her,' retorted Susan. 'But I'm not sorry. Why should I kowtow to her? I'm damned if I'm going to give that witch any satisfaction.'

Cyn looked her up and down. 'You're not the type to end up here. You're too posh. That's what she's got against you. She must think you're some kind of snooping spy. So, what's your story, then? Daddy wouldn't cough up the dough to get rid of it at some fancy clinic?'

Ignoring the question, Susan recklessly dug deeper. 'What happens to the babies that get sold? I mean, who buys them? Where on earth do they go? What kind of future life can they have if no one official knows what's happened to them? Who pays money for them and why, if the normal adoption agencies don't charge fees? It seems like real exploitation to me.'

Looking over Susan's shoulder, the other woman's face changed colour as she jumped down. 'Best not to ask, dearie,' she whispered.

Ashover had appeared in the doorway; how long she had been

there was unclear. A few yards behind her in the corridor lurked Bertha, unseen by anyone so far.

'Scram!' shouted the matron to Cyn, who vanished down the corridor past Bertha.

Then Ashover pressed her cold face hard against Susan's, cheekbone to cheekbone, as she shoved her into a corner of the laundry room. 'I'm going to wall you up, bitch, for your big mouth. And don't think your belly is going to protect you for too long. I've a doctor pal who could cut that kid right out of you, with me doing the stitches. And I can guarantee you won't like my needlework one bit.'

Susan's neck was gripped by a pair of sharp-taloned hands applying perfect pressure on the carotid arteries before she could open her mouth to scream. She had the sensation of slithering as the floor moved towards her.

Bertha fled.

CHAPTER 11

When Lucy made a doomed attempt to see Susan again at Rake Hall a week after her first visit, it was not Ashover who opened the door but the office manager, Elsie. 'Oh, Temple has left us,' she said.

'She can't have!' said Lucy, her voice squeaking in surprise. Clearing her throat, she tried to take it down an octave. 'I mean, I'm her sister. She would have told me.'

Elsie's look was an opaque one. 'Well, she obviously decided not to, dear. We get all sorts here, and sometimes they have their own reasons for being a bit secretive. She went yesterday, and she didn't leave a forwarding address. Maybe she went back home. I'm sure you'll be able to find her, seeing as you're her sister.'

Winter had begun early. Patches of snow still lay on the ground from the night before and the wind was a wicked one with sleet in the air. But Lucy, stumbling slightly on the cracked paving stones as she made for the gateway, felt as if she were on fire.

When he arrived home that evening, Alfred Standen noticed his daughter's fretfulness. Her shoulders were hunched up in a grubby Fair Isle cardigan as she brooded over the small fire in the grate that should have been stoked properly.

Being houseproud was not one of his daughter's virtues, but Alfred always made allowances. 'Not like you, Luce,' he said. 'What's up?'

She drew breath and then decided to tell him. Her father could be trusted with secrets, having had enough of his own ever since the selfish mare had left him to manage things on his own. The neighbours still didn't know the full story. There was a resentful rage within Lucy that she tried to suppress every time she thought about her mother.

'Whew,' whistled Alfred after she finished. 'Poor girl. I thought there was something up, but I didn't want to ask, like. She had her guard up, didn't she? I've met undergrads like her, nose in the air but stumbling in the gutter if they don't watch out. Those Varsity men can be young demons when the drink is in them.'

'What should I do?' asked Lucy. 'I've got to find out if she's all right. There's a matron in charge who gave me the creeps when I went there first, and Susan might have got into trouble with her. I just don't believe she left no forwarding address.'

Alfred bent down to light a Woodbine from the fire, which was about to go out. His mother, the late Granny Standen, used to pare her corns quickly and expertly into a small bucket by the same fireside, watched with fascinated horror by the child Lucy. 'Can you ask any of her pals in Somerville?' he suggested eventually.

'She doesn't seem to have any there,' said Lucy. 'There's only one girl she likes, but she's a bit of a hermit. Susan's scout Hilda is a good sort, apparently, though it's difficult to know how far she can be trusted about something like this. She doesn't want the top brass to know, although I did think of asking one of her tutors, whom she seems to get on well with. Should I try to meet him and sound him out? His name's Lewis, Mr C.S. Lewis. It's just that he might have a bit more clout than us when it comes to making discreet enquiries.'

Alfred gave another whistle, at which he was rather good. 'Blimey, girl,' he said. 'I've read about him in the paper.'

'But how do we get a message to him safely? Anyone could rummage around among letters in his pigeonhole in the Porters' Lodge,' persisted Lucy.

Alfred gave her the smile she loved. 'Leave it to me, Luce,' he said. 'I know his scout.'

CHAPTER 12

Squirrel liked his job, but he didn't like the liberty-takers. Of which there were quite a few. Some of them acted as if they lived on a different planet – or 'ivory tower' as the saying went. He snorted at the very thought.

He exempted people like Mr Lewis from that category, especially because the don seemed to feel a certain sympathy for the scouts, what with all the laborious tasks they had to perform. Maybe that was because Mr Lewis didn't look that fit: he wasn't as portly as his brother, granted, but he had a high colour at times.

There were stories about the old lady he lived with, always asking him to fetch and carry for her. And all the huffing and puffing, when he once volunteered to help Squirrel to move an ancient set of drawers to get at the mousetrap behind them, was alarming to say the least. As far as the scout was concerned, the little buggers could lie there rotting forever until the whiff from the corpses started to compete with the tobacco. Better that, surely, than Mr Lewis do himself a mischief – Squirrel couldn't have that on his conscience. Besides, he was one of the best tippers on his staircase. Not for him the paltry ten shillings a term that some of the Fellows thought they could still get away with.

In the scouts' pantry at the bottom of the stairwell, Squirrel drew on a roll-up and pondered the little favour he had been asked to do. He never asked any unnecessary questions, especially if it was for a friend. Which Alfred was. What with all that Alfred had put up with over the years from that she-devil, according to rumours, he felt sorry for the man. And he liked him. If Alfred had his reasons, that was good enough for Squirrel.

But what made him curious about the favour was the method of despatching it. Why couldn't Alfred leave a note in Mr Lewis's pigeonhole at the Porters' Lodge as usual? Perhaps it was because he had such a lot of post anyway; it was always stuffed full. Unless it was that Mr Lewis refused on principle to answer a letter with a local postmark from someone he didn't know. There was always that possibility, since a lot of his postbag came from America. The ivory-tower brigade who went around with their noses in the air would just throw something like that away and not even bother to reply.

Squirrel concluded that Alfred might want him to put in a good word with Mr Lewis for some reason. Stubbing out his fag, he slowly rose from the rickety pantry stool. Stoically, he climbed the stone stairway to Mr Lewis's rooms, trying to ignore the lumbago that was playing him up so much these days.

He had been doing this job since he was fifteen, and it didn't get any easier, though it had been considered a big step up from working in Oxford's Covered Market, his only other option at the time. It's a young man's game, but so many of us are old codgers, he thought, sighing.

Squirrel didn't have a son to hand the job down to in the time-honoured tribal way of the scouting fraternity. If he was going in for it now, he thought, he might be tempted to work at the car factory in Cowley instead. Good wages there. Even though the old man had wanted him to follow in his footsteps as a scout, he wouldn't have said no to that kind of money. He wouldn't have been a servant either, so he'd have got a lot more respect.

At least Mr L. didn't expect to have his shoes polished at the crack of dawn like some cheeky buggers did. Perhaps, Squirrel reflected, it was because the don had served in the first war and then done his stint in the Home Guard in the one just passed. Blacking his own boots must have come as second nature to him.

Lewis turned to look at Squirrel with some surprise. The scout was a man of set habits who kept to his schedule like clockwork. 'Shouldn't you be putting your feet up on your afternoon break, Cyril?' he asked.

'Sort of, Mr Lewis,' hedged Squirrel. 'But there's something I've been asked to give you. It's a letter to you from a mate of mine, another scout.'

'Who is he? What's it about?' Lewis felt bewildered, being something of a creature of habit himself, and quite unused to receiving letters from strangers delivered by hand. There was, of course, the endless correspondence from the public, much of it transatlantic, that he had been getting ever since the wartime broadcasts, but there were regular jokes among the porters about needing a wheelbarrow to transport it all. And there was so much of it that needed a thoughtful, considered reply – especially from the women who had been cruelly treated by men.

'Don't know what it says, sir,' said Squirrel truthfully. 'Thing is, I can vouch for him – he's a good sort. I know him and his daughter very well. If there's something on his mind, maybe he thinks that you can help him, like. Might be something religious. It won't be a begging letter, sir – Alfred's not like that. But he's heard of you like everybody else has. You can't hide your light under a bushel these days, Mr Lewis.'

Lewis smiled at the quote, the biblical origin of which he was fairly sure Squirrel was ignorant. The scout was a twice-a-year sort of Anglican, attending church at Christmas and Easter, and showed no interest in Lewis's spiritual life, which was quite a relief. Wouldn't want my scout breathing down my neck with theological questions; the days are packed enough already as it is.

Squirrel, who had recently been elevated to head scout at Magdalen after years of loyal service, performed his duties diligently and seemed a pretty decent sort, which was all one wanted. Far better than having someone sly snooping around and disturbing all the papers on the desk. Not that he had anything to hide, Lewis reminded himself. It was all a bit of a mess, but it was his kind of mess, and he knew where everything was.

Warnie used to say that a wife would sort him out, but he was no nearer to walking down the aisle with anyone than his brother was. It was just Warnie's way of going on about what he saw as Minto's malign influence.

'This is it, sir,' said Squirrel, proffering a small, crumpled envelope that had clearly been used before – the paper shortages were still driving everyone mad.

Despite being a martyr to lumbago, the scout was out of the door and down the steps before Lewis had even found his paperknife under the clutter. That was one of the many things he liked about Squirrel: he didn't outstay his welcome. For that, Lewis could even forgive him his dangerously radical *Daily Mirror* habit.

'Dear Mr Lewis,' he read. 'I am the daughter of Cyril's friend Alfred Standen, and I'm writing to you in the strictest confidence about my friend Susan Temple, who I understand is a student of yours. I'm very worried about Susan's welfare. May we please meet at Joe Lyons on the corner of Cornmarket at a day and time of your convenience so I can explain? Please drop me a line at the address at the top of this letter. Yours sincerely, Lucy Standen.'

Lyons, eh? mused Lewis, who never went into town for tea – so much better in his rooms or at The Kilns while he tried to answer all his correspondence. Probably full of women, bound to be noisy. Well, new experiences are supposed to be good for the soul, and it would certainly make a change from beers with the Inklings at the Bird and Baby or the Lamb and Flag opposite.

What would they think of old Jack arranging an assignation with a young woman of all people? Charles Williams would have been in his element in such a female environment, God rest him, but Lewis couldn't imagine John Tolkien putting up with all the screeching. Judging by the excerpts from his Ring Cycle (as Lewis privately thought of it) that Tollers read out to the other Inklings in their Thursday evening meetings, he tended to put his female characters on rather too elevated a pedestal.

Although Lewis had to admit he rather liked the sound of *The Lord of the Rings'* girl warrior Eowyn, a spirited young thing of whom he hoped to hear more from Tollers' latest drafts.

As he waded through his never-ending fan-mail and tried to answer the spiritual, and sometimes marital, dilemmas of distraught pilgrims as honestly as he knew how, Lewis was beginning to discover an empathy for the peculiar problems of the other sex that privately surprised and shocked him.

At times he was a regular agony uncle, especially when he received a distraught letter from a wife whose husband had taken a mistress. Somehow women seemed to expect him in his wisdom to wave a magic wand on their behalf, perhaps because he had given them that impression in his books.

Susan Temple was not the only female student to have noted Lewis's outrage in his book *The Allegory of Love* at the churlishness of a fictional twelfth-century marriage in which a loyal wife was expected to keep watch overnight, hold the horses and cover her sleeping husband with her own cloak during their journeyings.

Then there was his heroine Jane in *That Hideous Strength*, so much more imaginative than her dullard husband Mark. For all Lewis's bluster in quoting John Knox's 'monstrous regiment of women', he seemed to have an uncanny understanding of their sex.

Those who knew him well put it down to his devotion to his mother, who had died so young, and to the nurse who had tried to dry his boyhood blubs in her place before he and his brother were abruptly sent away by their widowed father to boarding school in England; Jack was nine at the time. Others, more cynical, smirked and tapped their noses as if to suggest the old chap had a secret life that might even involve secret women.

Having replied to Lucy's letter in the affirmative with a suggested date and time, he set out at the arranged hour for Lyons. On the way, he saw a familiar face approaching with its usual smooth smile. Giving a little wave as if to ward the man off, he quickened his pace to show he had no time to linger for a few words with James Slade, Christ Church's junior proctor. Lewis always distrusted gush, especially over his so-called celebrity.

It was a relief to see Lucy seated on the left by the bow window near the front door of the teashop, as she had promised she would be. At least, he assumed it was Lucy: the young woman met his gaze immediately.

In this alien environment of hats and lipstick and high-pitched babble between what he imagined to be best chums or work colleagues, he suddenly felt like the proverbial fish out of water. Would anyone guess, or even care, that he was from one of the colleges? There was no one here from his world that he recognised. The Grand Café on the High was the town teashop of choice for college dons and students with wealthy parents.

Lewis's fame on the wireless gave him a certain invisibility, though he had been horrified when Tollers and their other Inkling chum, Owen Barfield, told him about the painting of him on the front cover of *Time* magazine two months earlier after the success in America of *The Screwtape Letters*.

Even worse was the accompanying article, 'Don v. Devil', which made Lewis shudder at the very thought. Apparently, he was considered by the Yanks to be some kind of celebrity Christian. But no one in Lyons teashop would have seen it, he assumed, or cared one way or the other. He had more faith in the common sense of the average man (or woman) than that.

The young person before him certainly looked the sensible type: short, sweet-lipped with wavy brown hair, a steady grey-eyed gaze and a self-contained air. Nothing of the artificial glamour girl. Instead, she reminded him of one of his favourite evacuees at The Kilns during the war, with her almost child-like directness. As he studied her further, it seemed to him that she was quite young anyway: 18, perhaps.

She rose from her chair and formally extended an ungloved hand, introducing herself.

'A happy coincidence that your name is Lucy,' he said, trying to put her at her ease. 'My god-daughter's name is Lucy. Perhaps you know that it comes from the Latin name for "light".'

'Thank you for seeing me, Mr Lewis,' Lucy said stiffly. Suddenly overcome by shyness, she was trying to conceal how daunting she found him now that the face whose profile she remembered so clearly from the Charles Williams lecture was looking quizzically at her across the table. Ridiculous, Lucy's inner voice chided her. He's just a man like the rest of them, even if he's as clever as his reputation suggests. Yet there was nothing highfaluting about his language; he spoke like anyone else.

In the hope of breaking the ice, she decided on an impulse to mention that she had happened to sit next to him during the Williams talk, only to regret it when Lewis looked astonished. He must have thought that she'd been following him.

'Well, that is another remarkable coincidence, I must say.

Charles was the sweetest man, and I am proud to have called him my friend. He was the kindliest presence of all among us. I miss him greatly, and I am very pleased that you were enough of an admirer of his work to go to his lectures.'

'I didn't know anything about his writing,' she admitted shyly. 'I just really liked him. He was very nice to me at the OUP even though I'm only a junior clerk there, so I wanted to go and listen to what he had to say.'

Lewis stared curiously at the girl, so different from the gaggle of show-offs who cooed and clapped at every utterance by Charles. Her revelation about his late friend's thoughtfulness towards a mere underling did not surprise him, and yet somehow it touched him deeply.

Trusting that she had said the right thing, she ploughed on bravely. 'I wanted to tell you, sir, how worried I am about Susan.'

'Well, that makes two of us,' said Lewis. 'She hasn't turned up to tutorials, and I don't know what to make of it because Miss Temple is usually so punctual and reliable. Have you tried asking at Somerville? I was thinking of doing so myself. May I ask how you know her? Are you an undergraduate too?'

Lucy hesitated, and then unburdened her heart about how she had first met Susan – and the reason why her new friend had moved into Rake Hall. There was a calmness about Mr Lewis at first that made her say more than she had intended, but then she began to sense an underlying consternation that he was politely trying to hide.

'What shall we do?' she said, as if they had become allies and needed to work out a strategy.

He drew a deep breath. 'My dear, this has all come as a great shock. I need to think about this.'

'But you won't forget about it? I know she won't have gone to her parents. She was adamant about that. Her father would be very disapproving, apparently: he's a headmaster and very much the martinet. She didn't want her personal tutor or the Somerville principal to know either. But we need to do something. We can't let it go. She might be ill and need our help.

'I didn't like the feel of the hostel when I visited her there – nothing I could put my finger on, just a peculiar atmosphere – and no one except me knows she was there anyway. Should we go to the police and report her disappearance? I just don't know how to do it discreetly enough so that her college doesn't know she's been staying there. She told them she was ill and had gone home to her parents.'

That was when it sank in that because of his seniority and status, she was somehow expecting him to take charge and look into it all.

She seemed to read his mind at that point. 'I know you've written thrillers, Mr Lewis,' she said in a remark that seemed like a nudge.

Yes indeed, he thought, but they were . . . science fiction. And what did he know of wayward young women in real life, apart from the admittedly fascinating sob stuff in some of his American fan letters? In his thunderstruck state, all he could think of was Mary Magdalene, poor soul, after whom his college had originally been named.

He could just imagine Tollers spluttering into his Varsity Ale over cheese sandwiches in the Bird and Baby's Rabbit Room, especially at the thought of old Jack setting out to play the gumshoe in a world he knew nothing about.

After all, the only real-life detection he had ever done was to smoke out cheating students by catching the odd plagiarism in their essays. And he didn't even *like* detective stories. He left that kind of thing to Warnie – or dear old Dorothy, who had very properly warned him off getting too entangled in the fate of a female student lest people suspect the worst.

Yet one of Lewis's American correspondents, a woman who was hoping to leave her violent husband and wanted spiritual support, had referred in her sad letter to a line by Franklin Roosevelt in his inaugural presidential address that had caught the public imagination: 'The only thing we have to fear is fear itself.'

In the end, what am I for? he thought.

He looked at Lucy's imploring face. Seeing surrender in his eyes, she gave a smile of relief.

CHAPTER 13

Minto mustn't know what he was planning. That was his next, and perhaps his most urgent, thought. It took a second meeting with Lucy in Lyons to sketch out the scheme that had occurred to him, with Lewis insisting they sit at a different table for discretion's sake. He even wore another hat, which made him feel rather like a stage magician.

For a so-called creature of habit, he was beginning to discover within himself a certain capacity for recklessness that he put down to the stifling nature of his regular heavy workload. After all, what had he got to lose? There were few things he feared except heights.

Rake Hall itself needed to be urgently yet quietly infiltrated and investigated for clues to Susan's whereabouts. It was the thought of Mary Magdalene that had given him the plan he mapped out to Lucy. She thought it was a good – if very daring – one.

'Won't Ashover smell a rat when you turn up, sir?' she said

tentatively. 'I mean, she might think you know each other from the university.'

'If I were one of Somerville's academic staff, that would be a different matter. The matron would rightly be suspicious of me, thinking I was inviting myself into Rake Hall to sneak around and look for one of my students. But she will have no idea that I, a mere man from another college, happen to be one of Susan's tutors. Outsiders don't know how the system works. By the way, please don't call me "sir".'

With a mounting sense of excitement that surprised him, he telephoned the hostel from a street kiosk. The phone was picked up by a sweet-sounding voice that seemed to purr down the line and identified itself as Miss Ashover. He introduced himself – no other way but to come out with it – and sketched out an audacious proposal to do his bit for Rake Hall's moral welfare.

By offering to give an uplifting talk, he pointed out that he was simply following in the footsteps of the long-serving late Victorian prime minister William Gladstone and his good works among fallen women.

In fact, he had no intention of shoehorning such words as 'moral' or 'sin' into his address – his plan for the talk was more along the lines of sympathetic counselling – but best not to let the woman know that yet, otherwise he would never get through the door in the first place.

He correctly anticipated that the proposal would be met with a stunned silence at the other end. After a long pause – had she fainted with shock? – Miss Ashover said, 'This is a remarkably generous offer, Mr Lewis. May I ask you to call round to discuss matters further? So far as I know, we have never had such a proposal before, so I will naturally need to talk to the governors about your plan. But please do outline your ideas to me in a letter; that would be very much appreciated.'

In fact, Jane Ashover had no intention of asking anyone's permission. If he were to address the inmates with improving talks on moral guidance, she wanted it to be an unofficial secret for now; there might, she calculated, be some money to be siphoned off the wealthy visitor. If she was correct in assuming that the BBC wartime broadcasts and the sales from his books had left him very well off, perhaps he could be persuaded to play the philanthropist. And from what she had read about this local literary hero in the papers, he had no wife and family to keep. Above all else, she wanted to establish how – and especially *why* – he had found out about Rake Hall. After all, he came from another world.

Lewis did not at all like the sound of governors being consulted, but, having ventured thus far, decided to trust to divine fate. Would he also have to get permission from Magdalen? The president might take a very dim view of 'St Clive' addressing a bunch of fallen women, especially if there were a danger of it making the papers. He could just hear some of the cattier Fellows tittering at the news. As for the wives, it didn't bear thinking about. He knew he was considered an old fogey at Magdalen, where they all seemed to be either leftie atheists or hard-boiled cynics, or both.

But there it was: he had promised Lucy he would try to help and so he must put his shoulder to the wheel. His instinct therefore was to say nothing to anyone in college for the moment, so he wrote a vague, carefully worded letter with no mention of official college approval and slung it in the postbox at the other end of the High rather than leaving it at the Porters' Lodge to be posted.

He had always believed in honesty, yet there was no harm, he reasoned, in being partial with the truth – until such time as it was safe to be completely open. As he walked rapidly away, he had an uneasy sense that somehow his little planet had ever so slightly shifted on its axis.

He had told Ashover that he had first come to hear of Rake Hall through Christian contacts, but on reflection, over a nicotine hit back in his rooms, he couldn't be sure from her response that she had believed him. People seemed to think that only their faces could give them away.

Instead of Lyons for their third meeting, Lucy suggested that Lewis come round to her home instead. Jericho! One of his old stomping grounds during the wartime night watches when he would tramp those dark little streets near the murky canal at an ungodly hour with a rifle he hardly knew how to use.

Before making his way to Nelson Street, he decided on a last-minute impulse to drop in on the cemetery hidden away in Jericho's main thoroughfare. He had not visited St Sepulchre's for several years. Whenever he did, that sad squad of ghosts always invaded his brain.

He had read somewhere that as the door to the unconscious swung open, a suppressed feeling might escape its human host in material form. After all, shell-shock victims were said to share the phenomenon of mental dissociation with mediums who claimed to commune with the dead. Trench dreams could summon up supernatural phenomena caused not by the shades of the dead but by the unconscious minds of the living whose obsessions could awaken ghosts.

Yet, that night of all nights, when he sensed that he was now bound on a path from which there would be no going back, he found it hard to resist the morbid temptation to go into the cemetery. "'Bear-like, I am tied to the stake and must stand the course',' he muttered to himself. And since he was in the Jericho area anyway, it somehow seemed fitting that he should pay his respects to the dead.

Even Warnie's beloved Wilkie Collins could not have evoked a more spectral scene than the one glimpsed beyond St Sepulchre's gatehouse. Its witchy archway perfectly framed the war graves, the avenue of yews flanking the footpath into the cemetery and the giant central chestnut tree that rose up where the track came to an abrupt end. If only trees could talk, Lewis thought, what tales these woody ancients could tell.

In the distance, just beyond the boundary, was the Eagle Ironworks, owned by a local family, but even the stolid presence of that little hive of industry didn't detract from the Gothic atmosphere of this tiny city of the dead. Yet there was also a wistful sweetness to the silent little community of headstones, wreathed in tangles of ivy, with squirrels their only neighbours. He lingered by one, which commemorated the sacrifice of a boy soldier from nearby Canal Street.

As he turned away, his peripheral vision seemed to detect a presence crouching by another headstone on the other side of the path. The moon was shrouded by cloud, so it was difficult to see clearly. He wondered whether it might be one of the unquiet spirits – God knows he was used to those – but he couldn't be sure. As he left, there was no echo of footsteps behind him.

Nevertheless, he looked round cautiously as he waited on Lucy's doorstep. A gaunt rag-and-bone man with his horse, cart and bell passed by, giving him a swift up-and-down before geeing the nag on to more promising prospects in the next street. By the light of a nearby street lamp, Lewis saw that the front doorstep was pale grey rather than white like its over-chalked neighbours. Not too hot on housewifery here then, thought Lewis. Well, that's fine by me.

At his knock, an alert Lucy opened the door as swiftly as if she had been hiding behind it.

Entering such a small house – not even a hallway since it opened directly on to the street – made him feel as oversized and clumsy as if he were in some kind of Alice in Wonderland experiment. Easy to heat, though – The Kilns was so damned draughty because of its size.

The reason for the change of meeting place became clear when Alfred, smiling shyly, got up from his usual fireside perch and shook his hand with the air of a man who wanted to impart a confidence.

'Dad knows someone –' said Lucy.

'It's all right, Luce. I can tell Mr Lewis myself,' said Alfred gently. 'Pleased to meet you, sir. Sit yourself down, and I'll make us all a pot of tea. I think there might be some of Lucy's rock cakes left, although you might not want to trust your teeth on them.'

Lucy, who had heard the joke a million times before, butted in as Alfred went into the scullery. 'The thing is, the scouts' grapevine has told Dad about a regular racket going on at Rake Hall,' she said. 'The cook buys black-market meat and sells it on to the neighbours. What I thought I would do is pretend to be a new customer who has heard about her supplies and get to know her. She might let me in at the back door, and I can try to sneak around if I get an opportunity.'

'Well, best to do it when your Miss Ashover is otherwise engaged,' said Lewis, considering.

'That's what I meant!' she said, eyes shining. 'While you're giving your talks! You can be sure she'll be sitting in on *those*. It's the perfect time to have a skulk round. After all, you'll have the matron watching your every move, but she doesn't even have to know I'm there.'

Lewis leant back in the rather lumpy old wing-back armchair that had been pulled up by the fire for him and lit a favourite Gold Flake. So, my speech will be a decoy for her search? The idea was so audacious that he found it impossible to resist.

'But since the matron has already met you when you first visited the place, you'll have to be very careful indeed not to be spotted by her – even if you have a plausible excuse as a customer. She'll wonder why someone calling herself Susan's sister is now paying the cook a visit to buy food when the office manager has already claimed that Susan has left. It will seem too much of a coincidence.'

Lucy fished out the reading glasses she always carried around in her bag. 'I was wearing these when I met Ashover. Dad says I look like a librarian in them.'

'What does your father think about all this?' he said, immediately regretting the remark.

She bridled. 'He knows I can look after myself, that I wouldn't do anything silly. He knows I'm worried about Susan. How else can we find out what's going on? It's the only chance we've got.'

He looked around the tiny sitting room papered in a design of faded green chinoiserie. To his inexpert eye, it seemed to lack the cosy touch that women were supposed to confer – although Minto was hardly the best example.

'I do hope I'm not inconveniencing Mrs Standen with my visit,' he remarked automatically. Although he still remembered his own mother so clearly, mainly from her invalid's bed with her sad eyes soft upon him and one of her hands cradled in his boy's paw, that sudden choke of yearning in him always caught him by surprise. That loving lament for Sir Philip Sidney came back to him: 'A sweet, attractive kind of grace . . . continual comfort in a face.' What a silly old fool I am, he thought.

'She left us,' said Lucy shortly.

'I'm so sorry to hear that,' he said, assuming it was a euphemism. 'It's very hard to lose one's mother. The grief is always there.'

'No,' she said emphatically. 'She was a real so-and-so. She had a lot of affairs and eventually left us, going off with one of her fancy men. I don't think that worked out well because later we got a few letters asking for money. No address, just a post-office box number, so we had no idea where she was living. We ignored them. And Dad couldn't afford it. Why should he give her money, anyway? She made her choice, and she left us in the lurch.'

It was such an unusual circumstance, or so he gathered from an experience limited to his postbag, that he stayed silent, fearful of making some blundering remark, especially with Lucy staring hard at a cracked piece of lino and clearly trying not to cry after all these years, for her father's sake. He had always found it so much more comfortable to write down one's responses to such things.

Since Alfred was taking an age to make the tea, Lucy decided to risk more confidences. Because she and Alfred preferred to keep to themselves in Jericho, there was no one to confide in, and the two of them had talked the subject to death over the years. 'I was 13 at the time. I had to look after Dad from then on, and he had to look after me.'

'But why . . . ?' asked their visitor, his mind wrestling with this alien image. Absconding fathers, yes, ten-a-penny . . .

'Because she was a self-centred cow,' was the abrupt reply, 'and probably still is. We haven't had a letter for a long time: we don't know where she is, or even if she's still alive.'

Alfred came back in with the tea at last, lifting the cosy from the pot like a magician pulling a rabbit out of a hat. A nice flourish, but it was obvious he was fully house-trained; he had simply wanted to make himself scarce to give their visitor time to relax.

'Lucy told you about the cook at Rake Hall?' he said, knowing his impulsive daughter as he did.

'Yes, indeed,' said Lewis. 'I am indebted to you, Mr Standen, for your wide-ranging information.'

Alfred inclined his head. In his experience, few of the gown lot had a clue about what was going on in the town, so the acknowledgement was gratifying. Lucy's plan for infiltration didn't seem like a bad one to him: Mr Lewis was a clever gentleman, so no doubt he would know how to proceed without putting his daughter into danger. The scout supposed that he probably gave talks to people all the time; it wouldn't seem that unusual. And for him to venture into a house of fallen women to do good works only showed what a fine Christian he was.

'How's the tea? I prefer it strong myself, which is why I let it brew. And I've got a little bit of ham put by if you'd like some.'

They talked pleasantries thereafter, mainly food-related in those dark days of a rationing regime with no end in sight, until it was time for Lewis to go for fear of Minto ordering a search party from her bed. Surprised at how easily conversation had flowed between them all, he stood smiling at the Standens from the doorway before leaving.

Lucy finally realised where she had seen him before: during the war on night-watch duty, marching slowly past when she lifted the blackout curtain of her bedroom window at the sound of men's murmured voices. One of the faces had looked up at that moment, and it was possible to make out his features by the light of a half-moon.

She took the memory as a good omen.

CHAPTER 14

He had always had a good instinct for peril, and there was something rum about the milky-pale face of Jane Ashover in the parlour of Rake Hall.

What was the name of that film with a close-up of a nun suddenly, and shockingly, painting her lips scarlet before going mad? Warnie had told him all about it after watching the film twice, entranced, in one afternoon on a loop at a local picture-house. *Black Narcissus*, that was it.

He couldn't stop talking about it, saying that it had all ended badly, as one might expect. Something about a clifftop, which made Lewis shudder with that mixture of fascination and fear he had always felt about a great void yawning beneath his trembling feet. Being an awkward fellow, he never quite trusted his balance.

'I feel compassion for these young women,' he said to Ashover. 'They have paid a price for their weaknesses, of course, but one should show a Christian spirit towards them and try to help them build a new life.'

The matron's almond-shaped eyes, fringed with bristly dark lashes, flickered. 'You are quite right, Mr Lewis. We are very strong on guidance here: the moral-welfare officers sometimes pay a visit, and we have group prayers several times a day when we ask the girls to get down on their knees for forgiveness.

'It's not thought appropriate to take them to church: parishioners would talk, and we don't want our haven to acquire an unfortunate reputation. So we keep them safe here, but we make sure that they know the difference between right and wrong.'

'Yet they are not the only participants,' he said gently. 'What about the men?' He watched her recoil, her sinuous body giving her the look of a beautiful snake.

'We have no men in here, apart from the occasional handyman or doctor who comes in. What do you mean?'

'I mean,' he persisted, 'that men have put them in this predicament as much as the women have themselves. Are they not also involved?'

She was about to reply when the office manager put her head round the parlour door. 'May I have a word, please, Miss Ashover?'

Left to himself, Lewis looked around at the sparse furnishings. Hard chairs only, no homely armchairs or nice squidgy settees. At one end, there was a glass-fronted bureau that displayed tiny bone-china figures of wood nymphs – or dryads, as he preferred to think of them – and shepherds as well as centaurs, those mythical creatures – half-man, half-horse.

That small display provided the only decorative detail. For all the woman's talk of this place being a haven, there was no concession to comfort in the institutional-looking room with its dull, red, flock-papered walls on which no pictures hung.

As for the dustiness, Lucy had told him that the girls were responsible for all the housework since no servants were employed there apart from the cook and scullery maid, who both lived in. Even if their time was approaching, they were still occasionally obliged to scrub the floors on their knees with bristle brushes and cakes of carbolic soap. The effort was considered good for them, not to mention for the balancing of the books.

It was a clever economy, he had to admit: saving money and souls at the same time. Yet the thought of them being forced to crouch down and char when they were big with child revolted him.

Lucy had told him that Susan speculated it might even be a drastic way of 'bringing them on' if they had gone past their due date. Rake Hall liked its births to be on time – or, even better, a bit early. It seemed as if the matron could hardly wait.

Hauling laden tin tubs down the main stairway was reserved for the early days of the first trimester as a deliberate object lesson, Susan had claimed, in how heavy babies could be – both inside and outside the womb. There's a diabolical ingeniousness, thought Lewis, to the way the punishment seems designed to fit the so-called 'crime'.

Ashover reappeared and sat down opposite him, crossing one luxuriously sheathed nylon leg over the other in a slow, smooth movement that produced a faint fabric hiss. It had surprised him earlier that she hadn't been wearing a formal uniform to meet him. Instead, her outfit was a short austerity frock with a hem that ended at the knee.

Like a man counting the hours to the Day of Judgement, he stared at the clock on the wall beyond her head while she smiled her sleek, closed-lip smile and then answered his earlier question.

'You're right that the men are indeed to blame as well, but we expect higher standards of women. For they are the superior sex, are they not, Mr Lewis?'

He sensed the mantrap in time.

'I would say that women transgress less than men in general. The great majority of crimes are mostly committed by the male sex, after all: violence, murder, the very worst of it. But I am not making a special pleading for women; far from it. We should all be accountable.'

The carmine smile widened in that tight way as if winched out of her. He wondered if she were self-conscious about displaying the kind of bad teeth that could spoil the looks of many a beauty.

'Precisely so, Mr Lewis. You and I think alike on these matters. These girls have given way to wicked desires, and they should be made thoroughly aware of their sins if they are to become good citizens in future. Their families have handed them over to our care. We are not so censorious, however, as other homes that are very strict in their admissions policy, only taking "first fall" cases.

'Some will only take girls of previous good character who have transgressed just the once. They don't want to admit those who have had more than one child out of wedlock, since they fear it might encourage a pattern of licentiousness.'

She paused and smiled tightly again. 'We don't ask those kinds of prying questions of these women. That would require a lot of checking with their families, but there is no need for that. We welcome them all, those waifs and strays who have to be set on the right path to keep them safe from danger.'

There was a hint of virtuous smugness in her voice. But why, he wondered, would this woman take on cases that other homes had turned down? It was not as if she seemed to have any charity in her. Instead, there seemed something calculated about such beneficence – and he resolved to mention his suspicion to Lucy.

They talked further until she seemed satisfied with the approach he outlined for his lectures. As he had anticipated, there was no more mention of getting the permission of the governors. Instead, there was a faint gleam about her that made him feel uncomfortable. Thank goodness that she didn't know about his regular habit of donating a sizeable proportion of his income to various charities. As far as he knew, no one did.

Before he left, she insisted on taking him for a tour round the small garden. Safely back in his rooms later, he wondered whether she had done it simply as an excuse to unlock a cupboard just inside the back door and ostentatiously wrap herself in a long white fox-fur coat before leading him outside. Travelling all the way up to her slim throat, its almost insolent contrast to his humble gaberdine made him shiver.

Don't try to corrupt me with your display, he thought, wondering how anyone could possibly stalk the streets of Oxford in such an exotic pelt. Perhaps this was the only place where she could wear such a thing without attracting comment in such times of austerity. Yet as they paced around, she talked of nothing but sin and redemption.

'We bring the girls out here for their daily constitutional,' she told him. 'As you can see, we're not directly overlooked by the neighbouring houses at the back, and our high trees protect us. It's important to guard their privacy.'

He noticed a couple of gaps in the poorly kept hedge round the perimeter but supposed that gardeners, being male, were not encouraged to work on the premises for long. Either that, or else it was part of Rake Hall's skinflint tendency to spend as little as possible on the place so as not to spoil the poor wretches inside its walls.

'We keep the outer doors locked for the same reason,' continued the matron. 'Our little community is vulnerable otherwise, although of course they are free to go after their babies have been adopted.'

'Is adoption the usual way for most of them?' asked Lewis, surprising himself with the question. These were deep, dangerous waters, and Ashover eyed him as they paced around.

'I have never known any of our charges approaching their due date not to opt for adoption in the baby's best interests. What other choice does a single woman of modest means without a man's protection have? How could she possibly support the child if she has to work and cannot afford the childcare?

'And think of the scandal, too, of being an unmarried mother,' she said with what looked to him like a smirk. 'No, in my long experience, adoption is the only way. Better for both baby and mother in the long run.'

She droned on, fired up with the rhetoric of her moral crusade. 'So we ensure they take their exercise in this garden – it's good for them as well as for the baby. We take the safety of the unborn child very seriously indeed, Mr Lewis. These girls have been subject to evil influences before they come to us, and it's up to us to turn them into pure vessels so that we can redeem their mortal souls.'

As she spoke, she sounded almost saintly. It was fortunate she didn't seem to be aware that *The Screwtape Letters*, which had made his name in America, literally played devil's advocate with the theme of temptation. One girl had even been expelled from her school for having a copy of the book, or so he had heard.

Why should I play the watchdog over other people's lives? was his final subversive thought as he came away from the place, stumbling slightly on the broken paving stones as Lucy had done before him.

He slept badly that night. The crushed faces of comrades still haunted him from time to time; that was the worst memory of all, their identities almost unrecognisably mangled amid the mud and mire but the bodies still twitching until the life had finally left them.

But even as that silent company of corpses began to invade his brain, he tried to force himself to be stoical. He never spoke about this. Contemporaries didn't want to dwell on such graphic recollections of battlefield carnage, while the younger generation was blankly unknowing. And why should they not be? He was a relic, he knew that. But when the second great global war came, the memories resurfaced as if it were yesterday, particularly when he was doing that damned drill round the backstreets and the night sky returned the phantoms to him.

A few days later, after suggesting to Ashover that he start his talks right away, Lewis put the hazardous plan with Lucy into action and gave the first address at Rake Hall while she was knocking at the side door.

Lewis had carefully timed the talk beforehand by going over his notes in his college rooms to make sure that it would last long enough to give Lucy as many minutes as possible to investigate the place.

Of course, he dared not employ the devilish irony he had used to such effect for the character of Screwtape on the theme of temptation. These women had certainly satisfied their desires – or, perhaps, the desires of their demon lovers. Neither was he going to recycle those wartime broadcasts on sexual morality. The celebration of the body with the matrimonial pledge of 'with my body I thee worship' – as opposed to the human tendency to exploit it – would be a subtlety too far for an audience like this, who would probably be expecting only lectures on hellfire and damnation. Not to mention Madam Ashover.

Instead, he decided to pursue a middle way, gently urging them to listen to the inner voice that would set them on the right path to independence.

The crowd had shuffled into the red-walled parlour. One particular face seemed to him as defeated – though in a different way – as those poor men in the war that they thought would end all wars. Physically intact, of course, but with all the hope gone out of it. Lewis wondered whether she was the woman Susan had mentioned to Lucy; she was certainly older than the others.

Dressed in an awkwardly cut utility suit, she seemed suffused with shame, not looking at anyone – least of all their lecturer. She was nervously gripping a pocket handkerchief in her fist as if it were some kind of lifeline, perhaps because she feared she might cry.

All very different from some of the bored-looking young things, one of whom stared challengingly at him as if to say, 'Who is this old buffer, telling us what to do?' Rather daring of her, considering that Ashover and Elsie were both standing behind him throughout and had a perfect view of all the faces.

He was relieved to be introduced simply as Mr Lewis, which both he and Ashover agreed was the best way. Without a dog collar, he could hardly play the preacher. She simply explained to this captive audience that he was a man of God with their best interests at heart. His celebrity was ignored. In any case, he thought it doubtful whether any of the women in the room would know or even care who he was. All for the best.

*

Lucy, meanwhile, was in the garden at the side door to the kitchen, being smiled at by a suspiciously well-fed cook. During those lean and hungry times, being overweight always looked suspect – unless your legs were swollen with dropsy from malnutrition or heart and liver trouble, such as Lucy's great-aunt Ivy whose ankle fat seemed to ooze over her shoes and made the poor woman waddle. If the cook were suffering from dropsy, it must be an unusually bad case.

'My parents are running short, and we heard you might be able to help,' Lucy said, using the recommended euphemism.

'Could be,' said the cook coquettishly. 'Depends what you want.

If you're not fussy, there's plenty of whale meat. The smell goes when it's cooked, so it will be as good as beef steak, especially if you want to make rissoles. Leave me a list and I'll see what I can do.'

Beyond the half-open side door was the noise of someone up to their elbows in washing-up water, banging plates and pots together with particular venom.

'Put a sock in it, Vera!' snapped the cook, raising her voice, and then turned back to Lucy with a smile again. Horribly aware that she must be quick, Lucy handed over her scrap of paper.

'How much?' she asked.

'We can come to an arrangement,' said the fat one comfortably. 'My name's Phyllis Brumley – call me Phyll. Pop round again and I'll see what I have.'

Relieved, Lucy retreated round the side of the building and blundered down the front path with her heart hammering against her ribs, hoping that she hadn't been spotted in the dusk by anyone looking out of the front windows. As an extra precaution, she was wearing her father's spectacles as camouflage, which meant she could barely see where she was going. Luckily the paving stones weren't icy that day.

As she slipped through the iron gate, she risked a superstitious backwards glance at the building. Inside, Mr Lewis was still addressing his captive audience in the beautifully articulated baritone drawl that seemed to reverberate richly around the room and that had already captivated millions of wireless listeners around the world.

*

He had thought it best to keep things succinct for this initial talk, just as he had done with the RAF boys – sending them off to war with God's blessing ringing in their ears, or so he had rather uncomfortably felt at the time.

After a ripple of half-hearted applause, the inmates were ushered towards the exit, none of them looking in the least bit spiritually improved by his address. To buy a bit more time in case Lucy was still engaged on her vital business at the side door, he lingered in the hallway to ask Ashover about the age range.

'As you might expect, most of them are ignorant teenagers,' she replied, 'although you must have seen that we do have one or two much older women. One is nearly 40, and another is 38. I don't know about the circumstances that led to their condition, but I do know that the older one comes from a very religious family – strict Baptists. It must have been quite a shock for them, poor souls.'

Quite a shock for the woman, too, he thought. The man must have let her down. Presumably she was hoping for a wedding ring, but a certain type of scoundrel usually makes himself scarce at the earliest opportunity. Or so some of his correspondents had told him. 'I shall pray for her. What is her name?'

'Johnson, Bertha Johnson. Her friend is trying to persuade her to go to Australia with her in the hope of marrying a lonely sheep farmer prepared to take on a woman with a baby. The government there is offering a ten-pound passage to immigrants. Preferably white people, of course, because they want to increase the stock.

'But I told Johnson that it really wouldn't be a good idea to go to a country with so many snakes in it. The poor thing once told me she hates the creatures: she's positively phobic about them, and there are some absolutely giant specimens over there.'

How clever this woman is at rooting out people's weaknesses, he thought.

'What will she do instead?' he asked, risking the flippancy of a rhetorical question to which he already knew the answer.

She gave him a long, considering stare as if wondering why he was wasting her time. 'As I've already told you, Mr Lewis, the usual.'

CHAPTER 15

What he really wanted to be was a police 'ghost'. That way he could properly infiltrate, like a will o' the wisp.

Detective Sergeant John 'Johnny' George had all the impatience of a youthful thief-taker determined to try out a new strategy. One of the problems with working in the provinces, however, was the inevitable resentment towards any Scotland Yard initiative, such as the so-called Ghost Squad.

Officially titled the Special Duty Squad, the undercover operation had been set up in London to get to grips with a huge post-war crime wave. All the shortages of food, clothing, booze and cigarettes were proving catnip to a new kind of bad boy that had been inadvertently trained up – and tooled up – by the army in the fight against Hitler.

A weapons amnesty for wartime firearms had been announced the previous year. Unlicensed pistols brought home as 'souvenirs' by Forces personnel were to be presented to Oxford City Police Station in St Aldate's by a certain deadline to avoid prosecution. Yet here we are, thought George, more than 12 months later, and loads of the buggers still hadn't been handed in – if our snouts are to be believed.

Lighting yet another Craven A, he contemplated his next move as he paced around the small and scruffy CID room at St Aldate's. After being based in South London all through the war and in the sour aftermath of scarcities that made many wonder who, exactly, had won in the end, he had put in for a sideways transfer to Oxford. Nothing wrong with being a big fish in a small pond, he told himself. You could make your name that way instead of getting lost in the Smoke, where no one had invited him to join the Ghost Squad yet.

After years of chasing looters and dodging bombs by living underground like an animal, it was good to come up for fresh air somewhere else for a change. London was full of bomb sites, gaping craters amid ruined buildings that looked like Victorian Stonehenges, where children fought juvenile battles with jagged lengths of wood and cut their scabby knees on shattered glass.

Something unfulfilled in him was drawn to the ancient university town that remained so miraculously intact. According to a rumour, Adolf had wanted to preserve it as his victory capital. And as George prowled round his new patch, he dreamt of bettering himself somehow. Daft, of course; he was aiming above his station, as his dad would have said.

It was a strange set-up here, what with the university bulldogs in their bowler hats behaving like a private police force within a four-mile radius of all the colleges. They were just proctors' officers, for God's sake, which in George's book meant servants. The bullers were supposed to be in charge of sorting out the students, but he'd already heard cheeky tales about them trying to lay down the law to the townies too. If he caught any of them taking liberties on his watch, he planned to come down hard on them. But then that was all part of the challenge if you wanted to make your mark in a place like this.

'How you doing, Des?' he said to his deputy DC Desmond Parris, who had been rifling through a mass of papers on his desk with no obvious success. Parris was older and larger, though not noticeably disloyal, which was a relief. Having settled a while ago for an easy life in a backwater nick where his ability to get on with everyone counted for a lot and even solved a few crimes, he was a comfortably unambitious man. Since he had also worked as a part-time firefighter during the war, he had earned a certain respect for doing his bit.

Yet because Oxford had been spared the blitz that decimated London, Parris had fared rather better than some of his colleagues who volunteered to fight and then ended up as names on the war memorial erected at the station the previous year. No one doubted the patriotism of his firefighting, however, which he burnished like a medal.

Parris scraped his chair back noisily from the desk so he could put his feet up. It was the time of day when ties got loosened and, in Parris's case, belt ponderously undone to give the gut a breather.

'I hear loads of bloody butchers have been at it again with the under-the-counter stuff. I could send some of the boys around first thing to catch them unawares, but it's going on all over the place – forging coupons, God knows what. It's not fair when everything's so scarce, makes it hard for everyone else. But the guv wants to keep it out of the papers because it's bad for morale, upsets all the people on the straight and narrow.'

'It's the housebreaking and factory raids that get my goat,' said George. 'Know what Adolf told Himmler to do with housebreakers before the war? He told him to behead the next half-dozen that were caught, so he did – and he didn't get any more trouble from that quarter.'

'Blimey, that's a bit strong,' said Parris automatically.

'Tempting sometimes with some of those bastards,' said the younger man, relaxing into a grin against himself. 'But we wouldn't want to imitate Adolf's horrible ways, would we? It's contagious, that kind of thing. Not what I joined the force for.'

Parris gave him a deep look. 'Some do, though,' he risked.

'Don't I know it. Rooting out the rotten apples can take almost as much time as tracking down the other villains. That's what I found on my old patch, anyway.'

'Not just coppers, either,' added Parris casually. 'A few dodgy ones in the colleges, I hear. Oxford may be posher than you're used to, but it's not a paradise. We have our villains here as well as in London, up to all sorts.'

'Where's the DI, by the way?' said George. 'He was in a real paddy yesterday about the crime figures, and I wanted to have a word.'

'On the warpath earlier, but he's gone home now to take the wife out to some top-brass do. He was grumbling about it all day because of having to dress up. It's to keep the mayor and the local editors sweet, just to reassure them we're doing all we can. I mean, what else can we do? They're even nicking the coal.'

The young detective stubbed out the unfiltered cigarette with a frustrated grimace. 'Sometimes I wish fags were on the ration. It would stop me smoking so many of 'em. Let's go for a drink then – no point hanging around here much longer. You can tell me all the latest about your missus and your nippers. I need some exciting news in my life.'

That was what Parris liked about George: the kid hadn't let his rapid promotion go to his head, over whose slicked-back hair with its movie-star side parting he rammed a trilby to make himself look older as he shrugged himself into a William Bendix-sized greatcoat that had seen better days. Probably inherited from his dad, reckoned Parris.

George's keenness might have been irritating had he been neater, but somehow that eluded him – he always looked as if he had got dressed in a hurricane.

His snub nose and general untidiness made him look younger than he was. At six foot, he stood out – even for a policeman. Only the Irish Gardaí, raised on potato diets, were taller. For a copper, that was both a blessing – it had helped to get him noticed in the squad – and a curse, especially for anyone who wanted to be a ghost.

He caught Parris looking up and down the full length of him as they left. 'Bet Himmler would have liked to lop my head off. By all accounts, he could have done with a few more inches,' he said, laughing.

Rain was melting the sleet on the pavements as they crossed the street to the Bulldog, which had become George's favoured watering hole ever since his transfer to Oxford. He liked its proximity to the police station. A toad-necked man was loitering nearby with a fag, his trilby pulled low. When he saw George, he lazily explored his right earlobe with one stubby finger, turned smoothly away and strolled up towards Carfax.

As soon as they pushed open the door, Marcia started pouring their usual. George beckoned her closer and said quietly, 'Seen our blue-eyed boy lately?'

She shook her head and smiled a complicit smile, though he trusted her no more than anyone else in Civvy Street. No point getting too pally unless there was information to be had.

His job made it difficult to meet women – there were always awkward questions to be deflected – but he was young enough to accept his fate as the cannon fodder that the force required. It didn't stop him taking a vicarious interest in the older men's domestic arrangements. As they leant companionably on the bar counter, supped their ale and talked in low voices, he looked at Parris and thought to himself, Lucky bugger with his home comforts.

George was billeted in a room in the single men's quarters on the top floor of the St Aldate's station. All the other men there were uniform, since he was the only bachelor in the local CID. Even in the mess room, it could be lonely. Despite his attempts at friendly overtures, uniform branch were a touchy lot who resented the privileges of plain clothes, such as the licence to linger in pubs for longer than uniform's regulation half-hour at a time.

He hoped to wangle permission to move into private lodgings eventually, but that carried its own risks with the public finding out what he did for a living and either wanting to know more, or not wanting to know him. And, as he kept reminding himself, an aspiring ghost needed to remain low-key.

'When did you first decide to start a family?' he said conversationally.

Parris shrugged. 'It was a bit accidental, actually. She was nearly six months gone when we got married. Her old man almost got the shotgun out when he heard. He was all for denouncing me to the chief constable, but I told him not to be so stupid. It was a civil matter, and we were going to get wed anyway, so where was the harm. She'd even chosen her dress, though it had to be let out quite a bit when we marched down the aisle. He took a lot of calming down, I can tell you – even threatened to pack her off to Rake Hall.'

'What's that?' Having done a fair bit of homework before arriving, George felt wrong-footed at the mention of an unfamiliar name in such a small city.

'You're new to Oxford, so you wouldn't know. Anyway, you're the wrong sex. That's where they put the naughty girls. It's just down the road from here, but it's hidden away, very discreet. We never get involved, of course. Up to the girls' families and the moral-welfare lot that run the place.' He paused and grimaced with a certain manly disdain for such a messy subject. 'Why would we poke our noses in? Strictly women's business.'

Why indeed? thought George, aware that Marcia's capacious chest was pressed rather too close to him across the small counter.

CHAPTER 16

To Lewis, a college sherry party always tended to spell trouble. For a start, one or two of the dons' wives – especially Clarice Pope – were notorious for circling him as soon as he appeared. Just as nature is said to abhor a vacuum, so a 49-year-old bachelor must be sorely in want of a wife – unless he were the type of man that shunned women's company, which Jack Lewis didn't seem to be. It was too bad of such a successful author and broadcaster to be so elusive on the matter.

Jane Austen got it right about the female gossips of this world, he thought. Because of the sheer boredom of their circumscribed lives, they cannot resist meddling in other people's affairs.

He was not unsympathetic. Men like him had their work to sustain them, yet their women, if not also likewise employed in the life of the mind, were condemned to fret their spare time away from childcare with idle suppositions, especially if the children had grown up and moved away.

Am I unwittingly giving out some kind of signal to the match-makers? he wondered as he watched Clarice motoring smoothly across the Senior Common Room floor towards him. Lewis read everything in her avid expression.

'How nice to see you again, Mr Lewis.' Her teeth were large and flecked with coral-pink lipstick. 'The weather continues shockingly, I see, though at least we have been spared any more floods. And let us hope and pray we don't have another winter like the last one. Perhaps you can put in a good word to the Almighty? We would be so grateful.' This last added with a coy upwards glance that made Lewis's own teeth rattle.

'I was glad to see your detective-writer friend Miss Sayers in the Common Room with you recently. Is she likely to come up again soon?' continued Clarice, something of a conversational racing driver who took the bends at the very highest of speeds.

'I'm afraid she is very preoccupied with her ailing husband, so she can't often get away,' he replied.

'So sorry to hear that. I should like to meet her again. As I'm sure you would too.'

Lewis felt like bowing and moving on, but there was no escaping one of academia's apex predators – a faculty wife – until he had given her something to chew on. Nothing substantial, of course: if Clarice only knew what he had been up to recently, Magdalen would have been verily set on fire as the news blazed through the quads.

He caught sight of Cubitt, a history don, over her shoulder and raised his eyebrows to welcome him over. Cubitt was equally nosy, wondering to himself if old Lewis really had a secret life or was just wedded to his writing, as they all said.

When *That Hideous Strength* had been published two years previously, the final book in his Space Trilogy had caused quite a stir in college circles: a fantasy thriller set in academia, with rather more sympathy shown for the plight of a bored and frustrated (and attractive) young faculty wife than appeared strictly seemly in a middle-aged bachelor don. And how on earth did he know about what went on in a marriage?

Everyone in Magdalen, not to mention several other colleges, had been trying to recognise themselves – or their rivals, enemies and wives – in the novel ever since.

Lewis was only too aware of the gossipy paranoia. Conversations would suddenly die as he walked past people in corridors, trying to ignore the significant looks that came his way. As for the college guessing game over who his characters had been based on, it must, he thought, have been rather like the speculation back in the 15th century about the original models for Magdalen's gargoyles, sculpted by mischievous stonemasons to immortalise their foes.

'Mrs Pope has been talking about the weather we've been having,' he remarked to Cubitt. 'Can't blame her for complaining. And we're all up in arms about the coal shortages. But I think you might have an answer to that for Mrs Pope? Your scout is a most resourceful fellow by all accounts.'

Before Cubitt's rheumy eyes could reproach him for being lumbered with Clarice, Lewis made for the door. Cultivating a reputation for eccentricity was always useful for a quick getaway, though he took care to smile apologetically at the president who was just arriving before walking rapidly back to his rooms. After all, he was known to be a beer man with an antipathy to sherry.

Lewis had taken a liking to Alfred Standen, with whom he had started to share the occasional discreet pint before the three-mile hike back to The Kilns via Addison's Walk. Minto surely couldn't object to him meeting up with another man, he thought wryly.

The two men never chose Alfred's usual haunts. Luckily there was no shortage of watering holes in which they could smoke and drink in companionable silence, interspersed with a little light chat that never strayed into the minefield of college politics. Sometimes Lewis wondered how Alfred coped at Christ Church, a college whose pinch-nosed senior proctor had a chilly reputation for laying down the law beyond all reason.

Most of the time, Lewis took comfort in his belief in humanity's innate goodness, especially after the horrors revealed in the papers and on the newsreels of the depths of depravity during the war that had just passed. Occasionally, however, his father's cynicism surfaced.

He knew that his image as a man of the people was used as a putdown by rivals in academia, the most envious section of British society. In his view, it was simply his plain way of putting things. Even his wartime radio talks had been designed to be as conversational as possible, the popularity of which had probably, he suspected, cost him the chair of English Literature at Merton College that he had hoped for earlier in the year.

Nevertheless, his status as a don meant he was still a race apart as far as the town side of Oxford was concerned, and they didn't usually take a drink with scouts. So it was best to try to keep below the radar.

He made for the Bear on the corner of the felicitously named Alfred Street – a joke between them – and patiently awaited

Standen's arrival to catch up with a story the scout had been telling him about a Dubliner friend of his in London who swore by
Gauloises and Gitanes.

'Reckons they're more sophisticated than English cigarettes, but
then he calls himself an internationalist, so he would go in for the
foreign stuff,' said Alfred, logically enough. 'It's quite an education
all round, being with Liam. He had a go at me for talking about
being "in a paddy" – says it's bigoted.'

'I would agree with him. It suggests that having a hot temper
is an Irish characteristic, but they're no more likely to lose their
temper in my view than someone with red hair, which is also
highly debatable. Of course I'm an Ulsterman myself, so I hope
I'm permitted to know what I'm talking about.'

Alfred smiled in his emollient way. 'Sorry to contradict you, Mr
Lewis, but I've known a few fiery carrot-tops in my time, especially
at school. But it could have been because they were always getting teased about the way they looked. Which comes first, eh? The
temper or the teasing?'

Lewis smiled back. 'These are deep matters for debate, Alfred.
Call me Jack if you like – let's ditch the formalities. What else does
your friend Liam say?'

'A lot. He's fluent all right. He's very well read, and he knows
so many people. He was telling me about a West Indian chap
called Hubert in his union chapel who had problems finding regular work in London after being demobbed from the RAF. Liam
thinks he should come up here to the Cowley plant because the
unions are very strong there.

'He got friendly with Hubert because they were in the same boat when it came to finding digs – signs in the landlords' windows that said, "No blacks, no dogs, no Irish." The cheek of it, comparing men and women to animals – it's a disgrace.'

'I've become quite the cat-cherisher myself,' said Lewis, 'but I can see your point. Personally, I would detest any landlord or landlady who banned dogs and cats as well as human beings. But maybe I'm an oddity for liking noble beasts. Some animals are definitely more intelligent than others; you could almost imagine them capable of speech.'

Alfred nodded sympathetically. 'A word of warning, by the way, Mr Lewis. If you're fond of the moggies, be on the lookout for skinned cat served up as skinned rabbit. They're very similar when the head and the fur's off, but the way you can tell the difference is that the rabbit's kidneys look a bit out of line – they're offset, like.'

Lewis stared at him, perplexed. The idea of such a diabolical switch by unscrupulous butchers had never occurred to him. Could the cooks at Magdalen have fallen prey to it? Rabbit was such a useful staple, given the meat shortages, that the notion of killing household pets and passing them off seemed peculiarly wicked to him.

Probably some blackguards were taking advantage of the excess kitten problem. But there was such a lovely, questing intelligence about cats, despite the tiny facial muscles that made them look so impassive, that he found them impossible to resist.

After taking a large gulp of very agreeable India pale ale, he decided to change the subject. 'Why did your friend Liam move to London? It must have been much quieter in neutral Ireland with fewer bombs to contend with.'

'The usual Irish curse of unemployment. Also, he upset the local Catholics in Dublin, apparently. Told me some funny stories about him and his rebel friends forever dodging the Catholic Action squad, who used to try and beat them up in the street whenever they marched around with their banners, campaigning and whatnot.'

'What were they campaigning about?' asked Lewis, beginning to feel that his own education in the university of life had been sorely lacking till now. But then current affairs had never been his strong suit.

'The convent laundries that use girls as unpaid labour. No one dares say anything because they've got the Church's backing.'

'How do they get away with not paying the girls for their work?'

Alfred cast an indulgent look at this innocent man of letters. 'Because the girls are regarded as the lowest of the low for having babies out of wedlock, Mr Lewis. They give birth in the convents, their babies are taken for adoption, and then the poor sods are put to work in the laundries as a penance.

'Liam told me that a lot of them are in there for years – and some of them never even come out at all. Says it's because they get institutionalised.

'It's much harder for women like that over there, he says. It's a much smaller population, and everyone knows everyone else's business. You can't hide the scandal easily.

'So, rather than end up in the laundries, a lot of the Irish girls come over on the ferry to have their babies and get them adopted over here before their parents even find out they're expecting.

'It's been going on a lot since the end of the war when the

government lifted the travel restrictions with Ireland. The women give some excuse about looking for work in England. Of course, some of them stay on here for good. Why wouldn't they? It's a nicer life over here in my opinion. We're not so ruled by the Church.'

He shifted on the bench, prudently lowering his voice in the quiet pub. 'Liam told me that sometimes it means a shortage of kids to adopt back in Ireland, and there's a big market for them.'

'A lot of country folk can't get wed until they've inherited the family farm. By then, they're often too old to start their own families so they have to adopt a child, even if it's just to have some help on the farm – more like slave labour in some cases, I'm told,' he added with as much cynicism as Alfred would ever muster.

'And then there are the Yanks as well. Queues of them apparently, all wanting pure white Irish Catholic babies. They pay the nuns a lot – disguised as donations, of course. God forbid that the kids should end up in Protestant families over the border in the north – the nuns would rather send them to America instead, or else Australia or Canada. I hear lots get sent out into the countryside there to work their guts out, poor kids, and probably not even going to school much, either. It's a real old export business. I call it scandalous.'

Lewis brooded as he listened. Back home in his bedroom at The Kilns, he had hung a 17th-century map of Ireland by the Dutch cartographer Joan Blaeu which depicted an ancient hierarchy in the colony that still seemed to hold good.

Two images of the magnificently accoutred Gentleman and Gentlewoman of Ireland were at the top, followed by the bourgeois Civill man and Civill woman of Ireland, and then at the bottom – these last two well beyond the proverbial pale – the Wilde Irishman and Wilde Irishwoman, both skulking under what looked like animal hides rather than cloaks.

He tapped the remnants of ash out of his pipe before dropping the first pinch of fresh tobacco into the chamber. Next to him, Alfred was rolling another cigarette.

Were he ever given the choice, he hoped he would have the courage to opt for wildness out of sheer devilment and join the ranks of the rebels like Alfred's young friend.

CHAPTER 17

For his second evening lecture at Rake Hall, Lewis had decided upon a Christmas theme to emphasise how the place had given shelter to mothers and babies in the very best Christian tradition. The message was met with a stony silence by the modern-day Mary Magdalenes. Perhaps, he reflected, they were depressed by their supposed safe haven's complete absence of Christmas cheer: not even a dilapidated paper lantern or two.

Ashover, however, seemed pleased – animated, even, beyond her usual studied calm. 'Thank you so much, Mr Lewis,' she murmured after helping Elsie to usher their sullen charges out of the parlour door. 'May I have a word?'

They sat down in front of the cabinet with its strangely poignant little porcelain creatures, frozen forever in their bone-ash attitudes. At first, he listened with only half an ear, conscious that Lucy might still be at the side door.

'You have been such an inspiration to my girls, Mr Lewis,' she said smoothly. 'And I do hope that we have made you welcome. Would you like some tea? I could ask Cook to bring a pot.'

'Please don't trouble yourself, Miss Ashover,' he said quickly, not wanting any disruption in the kitchen.

'Oh, it's no trouble, I can assure you. It's a cold evening outside, and we want you to feel at home here. Cook is famous for her fruit cake, which she conjures up from almost next to nothing. I'm sure we can tempt you.'

She rang a little bell, and after a few minutes a stout party in an oilcloth pinny put her head round the door. 'Phyllis, please bring us tea and cake,' said Ashover to the bleary-eyed cook.

He guessed he was getting what passed for the royal treatment in this flyblown place. It flummoxed him, not having expected his audacious plan to work so quickly and so well in such dangerous circumstances. She's buttering me up, he thought.

Then she moved in for the kill. 'Mr Lewis, your two talks have been so beneficial that I feel you are almost one of us now. I do hope that you may give more lectures when you are able. We are a modest little organisation, however, so perhaps we might seem rather undeserving.'

It would have been impolite to say anything other than 'Not at all, Miss Ashover.' Then he fell silent, cursing himself for having given the creature her opening.

'In that case, might I prevail upon your great charity, Mr Lewis? We are very much in need, and if you were able to keep us in mind for a donation, we would be so grateful. You have seen for yourself how things are here: we have to pinch the pennies, and it's so hard on the poor young women, who really are deserving cases.'

Hoist with my own petard, he thought. Yet she forgets I've seen her arrayed in her monstrous fox fur, which must have cost a king's ransom.

'That is a most interesting idea, Miss Ashover. I will give it very serious consideration. Were I to go ahead, would you be able to put me in touch with your governors?'

Touché. It was his turn to land a hit. For a split second, the creamy mask slipped. But she recovered, returning to the attack.

'Yes, of course, Mr Lewis. But I'm wondering' – she hesitated and smiled – 'would you want to be identified, may I venture to ask? Some donors prefer anonymity, of course, especially if a gentleman were to be troubled about the risk to his reputation by visiting a place like ours. You might prefer to make your involvement with us a private matter.'

There was a razor sharpness to her gaze. 'After all,' she added almost conversationally, 'people can be such gossips. And they may speculate quite unfairly about a gentleman's personal motives. It seems to me that bachelors are particularly vulnerable to rumour.

'But please don't worry, Mr Lewis: I will keep everything absolutely secret so that we can enjoy a very fruitful relationship.'

*

Lucy's return visit to Rake Hall's side door during Lewis's second talk had been cut short when Phyllis Brumley, who liked to indulge in lengthy chats on the doorstep, heard the summons of Ashover's bell. 'That's Madam cracking the whip – I'm always on the trot,' she grumbled.

Sending Lucy away with an unidentifiable slab of animal

wrapped in greaseproof paper, she urged her to call again on the off-chance. 'Everything depends on my suppliers – it varies from day to day,' she said with a sly look that suggested myriad murky sources. Off the back of a lorry, probably, thought Lucy.

Two days later, she decided to risk another visit to view the available contraband, since Alfred was quite the meat-eater when he got the chance. This time she wore a headscarf but no spectacles – either hers or her father's – to lessen the risk of being recognised by the management.

The door was opened not by the cook but the scullery maid – she who sounded as if she had been up to her oxters in washing-up water, her mood as filthy as the liquid, when Lucy had called round on her first visit. She looked sleepy.

'Mrs Brumley's not back yet,' she ventured. 'Did you order something?'

'I gave her a list, and she said she would sort something out,' said Lucy. She felt the maid's gaze wash over her, and then the unexpected happened.

'D'you want to come in and wait? She's gone to the Covered Market so she might be a while.'

As soon as Lucy crossed the threshold, she realised the girl's game.

She was already filling two glasses. 'I'm Vera. Keep me company,' she said, raising one of them and sitting splay-legged on a stool. Lucy had never drunk whisky before but perched rather gingerly on a second stool in the dingy little scullery and decided to give it a go. Her throat felt as if a firework had been thrust down it.

'Down the hatch,' said Vera with another flick of her wrist. 'No point in wasting it. Good stuff, and more where that came from.

Have another.' She smiled companionably at Lucy. Her skin was slightly muddy-looking and the eyes green and watery, almost as if she had amphibian blood.

Lucy put it down to the fact that she probably rarely left the scullery to see daylight. What with all the dishes piled up in the sink and a floor with plenty of wet patches as testimony to her workload, it was a wonder she didn't have webbed hands and feet.

'You look like a good sort. Not the kind to get herself into trouble like this lot here. Want me to show you around? I know the place inside out. Go on, have another.'

'I don't want to be a nuisance,' gasped Lucy, still aflame.

'You're not. I like a bit of company, but I'm not supposed to mix with the bad 'uns. They look as if they could do with cheering up, but I'd get sacked if I so much as offered them a drop. Even at Christmas. And I need this position.' She looked so glum that Lucy almost felt sorry for her. What was the point of being a soak without someone to share it with?

The scullery walls were painted with green distemper, which toned rather well with Vera's complexion. Even Lucy realised that the floor could have done with a good scrub of carbolic soap. Next to the old butler sink was a cupboard. Judging by the grubby fingermarks round the door handle, Lucy guessed that the supplies of booze were kept in there.

Opposite was a pantry, its door ajar. It seemed to house most of Rake Hall's comestibles and other stores. Lucy noticed that it also contained a large, scuffed refrigerator. Better than Dad and me, she thought ruefully. They had to make do with their old outdoor meat safe.

Beyond the scullery was a larger room: the kitchen proper, with a long wooden table and rows of utensils hanging from both walls. Everything looked worn and chipped. It was a typical cookhouse of the institutional sort, though no more dismal than most by the standards of post-war austerity.

Lucy found herself wondering what the Oxford college kitchens were like. Alfred had once let slip that although dining in Hall on those long polished tables with rows of oil paintings overhead looked all very fancy, the cooking facilities behind the scenes weren't much cop.

'Come on,' urged Vera, standing up unsteadily. 'Let me give you the royal tour. It's Elsie's afternoon off, though I can't show you upstairs – Madam Ashover would have my guts for garters. I heard her go up to the birthing room a bit earlier to help out,' she added, 'so she'll be there a while; Gawd help the poor mother she was going to see, that's all I can say.'

Lucy followed her through the passageway to the hall and watched as she produced a tiny key from her stained overall pocket to unlock the office. 'It's Brumley's,' she whispered. 'She has spares for all doors, and I know where she keeps them.'

The room was dominated by vast filing cabinets against one wall and a large desk with a typewriter. Next to it lay a ledger. 'Elsie keeps the other book in her top drawer, which she locks. She likes to boast that she keeps her really important keys in her corset – one of those wartime ones with a hidden pocket, so you didn't need to carry a handbag that might get dipped by pickpockets in the blackout. She only takes that off once a week for her bath.

'But I can always pick the lock if I want,' said Vera airily, sitting on the edge of the desk and taking another swig. 'One of the girls here has a brother doing time who taught her how. It's easy.'

The skivvy cocked her head sideways, looking at Lucy. A message was being passed on – but what?

'I like you,' said Vera largely, looking her over. 'You're nice and quiet. I can't stand the caterwauling types who can't take their drink. You have to be like the men, that's the way to approach it: hold your liquor like they do. Come again. I'll show you more.

'But let's go now, because old Brumley will be coming back soon. I can usually time her visits to the market like clockwork, but there's always a chance she hasn't got what she needs if something ... if the supply chain has gone wrong. Then she comes back early. You can never predict.'

Assuming that she was referring to illicit stuff, Lucy followed Vera back into the scullery and the half-open door that led to the arctic wastes outside.

'Have another one for luck,' Vera urged, fixing her green eyes on her. 'You're a pal, you are.'

Lucy valiantly poured another liquid firework down her throat. She found herself hoping for Vera's sake that the latter's breath wouldn't betray her when Phyllis Brumley came back.

It was not until later, when she was back in bed in Nelson Street and stirred into wakefulness by a slight noise outside in the street, that she sat bolt upright with a sudden realisation.

She, who had wrestled so long with the Kalamazoo, should have twigged hours earlier if only she hadn't been so sloshed.

CHAPTER 18

Against all his instincts, Eddie Jarvis had become obsessed with watching the little ledger queen at the Oxford University Press.

He resented the way she studiously ignored all the boys in the basement whenever she went down there. Who did she think she was? Nothing much, judging by her shabby clothes, but there was an air of independence about the tomboyish Lucy that puzzled and maddened him. She was the only female there. It was not right that she should behave as if she had a secret that set her apart with that slow smile of hers.

Never mind. He had a meeting with the bulldog later, and he always felt more of a man in Fetch's company. There were plans afoot, and Fetch had started to call him by his first name, which was a good sign. Not Edmund, which he hated, but Eddie.

'Get ready, Eddie,' Fetch would say with a grin.

I'm ready all right. Anything you can throw at me. He licked already-wet lips.

As they sat nursing pints in the Lamb and Flag one evening, the bulldog said quietly, 'I want you to start doing deliveries in Jericho. There's a woman who orders stuff regularly from us. There's a bigger job coming up, too, but I want to make sure you're up to it first. Very hush-hush.'

He leant forward until one hank of brilliantined hair nearly brushed Jarvis's forehead, which was festooned with pimples. 'I need to know if you can look after yourself, sonny.'

Jarvis bridled. 'I can take care of myself. I'm all tooled up, if that's what you mean.'

'What with?'

'I always carry a razor.'

'Have you ever used it apart from attacking that fuzz on your face?'

The boy looked sulkily at him. 'Of course. I had to give one bloke a bit of a scratching; he won't mess with me again.'

Fetch looked sceptical. He could count on one hand the number of ferociously scored faces and necks he'd seen in the backstreets of a small place like Oxford. Not like the East End, where it was a badge of honour among some to wear a slash or two. Made you look like a hard man.

He had managed to save his own skin from a going-over by the razor gangs, but then he prided himself on being quite the ducker and diver. A bulldog had to look respectable to do his job.

But he needed to know if the kid was up to it.

'Fancy a bit of weekend travel?'

'Where to?' said Jarvis suspiciously.

'I can't tell you at the moment, but there's quite a bit coming up.

Thing is, you got to be flexible. And I need to know if you can be the big man. I need someone with plenty of fight in him. You can't mess around – you've got to get in there. You told me that you liked the drums, that you've played with a few local bands? That's what's given you a bit of muscle?'

Jarvis considered, leaning back on his bar stool and adjusting his cuffs. 'I did a Saturday job at a butcher's while I was at school – that's what built me up a bit. All that chopping meat was pretty useful for the drums, as it turned out – very good for the biceps.'

The full beam of the blue searchlight was fixed bright upon him, followed by a yellow shimmer of teeth.

CHAPTER 19

Turning right from St Aldate's into the High, DS George thought at first that he had seen a phantom. Someone who looked just like Detective Inspector John Gosling, a key member of Scotland Yard's undercover Ghost Squad, appeared to be crossing the road in front of him instead of walking down some mean London backstreet in pursuit of his latest quarry.

Almost immediately, George realised his mistake.

This man was a few inches shorter than Gosling, who was 6 foot 1. But apart from that, they had astonishingly similar features, with the same shaped eyes and receding hairline that gave them a distinctive domed forehead, not to mention the same burly countryman build that had earned Gosling the affectionate nickname of The Yokel.

Having come from farming and haulage stock, he was reputed to be the strongest and bravest man with his fists that the squad had ever recruited. Whenever George glimpsed the great man from afar in the corridors of the Yard, he would gape at him in awe.

Gosling had a reputation for being shrewd, humane and kind. Police canteen gossip would marvel at the occasions when he had been known to slip a miscreant's wife a few readies from his own pocket to help her out when her old man got locked away at His Majesty's Pleasure. Cynics said it was a calculated move to recruit her – or even her husband after he'd served his time – as a snout. More charitable colleagues argued that it showed a commendable Christian understanding of a wife's desperate predicament when the wage-earner was banged up inside. Whatever his motivation, Gosling was undeniably a one-off.

On an impulse, George followed the lookalike, quickening his pace until he was alongside him. 'Sorry to bother you, sir,' he said quickly, showing him his ID.

'What is the matter, officer?' said Lewis, startled to his soul at being stopped by this tall young stranger with gaunt cheekbones who looked at him with appraising grey eyes. For all he knew, his secret visits to Rake Hall might have transgressed some arcane criminal law quite unknown to Oxford dons. 'May I assist you?' he added prudently, about to fish in his breast pocket for his own identity card.

George smiled to put him at his ease. 'Nothing to do with any investigation, sir. Or, at least, not a criminal one. I was just wondering if your name was Gosling, if you were related to one of my former colleagues in London. It's just that you're the absolute spit of him. It would be quite the coincidence to see him fetching up in Oxford, unless you were his brother or cousin.'

'No,' said Lewis, trying to hide the sense of relief that was sending his adrenaline sky-high. 'No Goslings in my family, I can assure you, officer – not even a Goose. My name is Lewis, C.S. Lewis. I'm known to my friends as Jack.'

'You do look remarkably like him,' said George. 'I apologise for having troubled you, sir.' The man's accent had disarmed him – he was not yet experienced enough to be cynical about the well-spoken types. With the copper's habit of covering every angle, he couldn't resist adding, 'I hope I haven't delayed you in anything?'

'Not at all. I'm just making my way back to Magdalen College for dinner,' said Lewis hurriedly, feeling that somehow he had to explain himself (and upbraiding himself for such absurdity). 'I'm one of the Fellows there.'

They politely tipped their hats to each other, and Lewis continued along the High, still feeling faintly nervous with the eyes of the law on his back. Watching his progress along the street, the detective resolved to make discreet enquiries. The name meant nothing to him, but it had fired his imagination.

One of the university Fellows, eh? What a gilded life they must lead with their dinners and their gowns and their ceremonials – not like ordinary fellows, pounding the streets in pursuit of a never-ending supply of villains. Probably a scholar like that had never encountered human wickedness in his life.

He mooched thoughtfully on his way. Bet old Gosling would be put out to know that someone with his face and his build was walking around Oxford, bold as brass. Ghosts liked to keep a low profile, even if they were 6 foot 1.

CHAPTER 20

Lucy could hardly wait to tell her co-conspirator about the concealed ledger at Rake Hall – and her suspicions about its purpose.

Although Vera claimed to be able to pick the lock of the drawer where Elsie kept the ledger, that could have just been the oceans of drink talking. For any investigation, they would need to make sure Elsie was safely out of the way.

When in turn Lewis mentioned how he had been stopped by a policeman in the street earlier that evening in a case of mistaken identity, an already-jumpy Lucy, who did not generally believe in coincidences, was immediately wary.

'Not that I've had much to do with the constabulary in this city,' Lewis said mildly, 'but this young man struck me as trustworthy. Something about the eyes. I've found the snake pit of academia to be very good training for character assessment: it's don-eats-don in our world, believe me.

'If we get into a jam with this business, Detective Sergeant George might be just the young fellow to help us out. I know Susan wanted you to keep everything hush-hush, but we can't discount the official channels completely – and we might need them soon.'

Meanwhile, it was decided between them that Lucy should try another reconnoitre of Rake Hall by placing an order of rabbit – or what she devoutly hoped was rabbit – with 'Call-me-Phyll' Brumley. Lewis seemed so impressed by the daring shown so far by Lucy in her explorations that she hadn't the heart to mention how much drink had been involved.

*

The side door was opened by her improbable new chum Vera, whose eyes gave a glistening welcome to a fellow carouser. Without being asked, Vera explained about the cook's absence as they settled down in the scullery for the inevitable.

'She's had words with the matron,' Vera said. 'They often have a ding-dong, but Ashover will always be the top dog around here. So, when they've had one of their spats, Phyll goes off to see a mate of hers and drown her woes. Mostly it's just to annoy Ash, who likes her to stick around. Phyll pretends her friend is ill and she has to go and see how she is. Ash knows it's a lie, but she also knows she can't push Phyll too far, so she cuts her a bit of slack from time to time.'

Are they all heavy drinkers in here? thought Lucy. She supposed the place must drive them to it. Tentatively, she asked, 'What do they argue about?'

Vera downed another shot. 'It's all about divvying things up. Phyll doesn't get her fair share, so she thinks. But Ash needs her help so she strings her along. It's hard to manage on wages here, I can tell you. In fact, Phyll owes me something right now, so I'd better just open another bottle instead.' She gave an impudent grin.

Lucy couldn't help grinning back while wondering just how much more firewater she could consume in one session without keeling over. Surely this was the moment to bring up the subject of the locked-away second ledger while the scullery maid was nicely blotto. She sensed that very little praise or thanks ever came Vera's way, so a bit of gush might go down well.

'I'm surprised they don't give you a rise. You really seem to know what's what round here,' she ventured. 'You're wasted on all that washing-up – you'd make a good supervisor.'

'Ooh, I would, believe me,' smirked the other girl. 'I got my spies to keep me informed. Want to have a butcher's at the real ledger I was telling you about? We've got a bit of time – Ash is seeing to some new girls upstairs and Brum'll be woozy when she gets back anyway.'

'But what about the office manager?' asked Lucy.

'Elsie would be down on me like a ton of bricks if she knew. But she's been having trouble with her toothy-pegs lately, so Ashover let her go to the dentist this afternoon. She'll probably have to have a couple of them out, and that will cost her an arm and a leg. Better to just tie a bit of string to a door handle and give it a good yank, if you ask me.

'She's been guzzling too much sweet stuff – and of course we know where all that lot came from. "Be sure your sins will find you out",' Vera intoned, shutting her eyes for a second or two.

Within seconds, they were inside the office again. Breathing heavily in a way that seemed to match every amplified beat of Lucy's heart, Vera removed a hairpin from her rather slummocky Victory Roll 'sausage' and picked the lock of the desk's top drawer, carefully aligning the pins in the cylinder to rotate the inner chamber.

Having successfully breached the drawer's defences, she brought out a scuffed leather-bound book and heaved it open for the other girl to read the transactions. Long lists of surnames, dates, prices and some kind of code. The letter C seemed to feature rather a lot. Lucy's finger traced the italic script thoughtfully as she turned the pages.

Vera watched avidly while keeping a lookout. 'It goes back a long way – six years all told, as long as Brumley and Ash have both been here,' she whispered. 'They've made a packet, they have, especially during the war when so much else was going on. Better close it now, though – Ash will be down soon. We'll hear her before she starts coming down the stairs because there's a spot on the landing that really creaks.'

The further back Lucy looked, the more faded the writing. She was about to close the book and give it to Vera to lock away again when among the entries for 1942, she saw, with a jolt that made her feel sick to her stomach, a familiar surname.

CHAPTER 21

A brutal blow across his face nearly knocked him sideways.

'Don't you dare disrespect me, you lout. I'll give you what for.'

The woman glared at Jarvis while Fetch grinned in the background. Wouldn't do any harm for the boy to know who he was dealing with.

Ashover was stronger than she looked after years of hauling patients in and out of bed and all the other things that nurses had to do – especially those in asylums, where the pay and the status were historically low but some of the staff ruled the roost as compensation.

'Bloody hell, you nearly broke my jaw,' mumbled Jarvis, tasting blood in his mouth from the collision between skin and teeth.

They were in a small, dingy warehouse off the Cowley Road. It was around 11 p.m., and Jarvis had been helping another man, a taciturn fellow, to drag knobbly sacks full of valuable plunder from the coal merchants in Hythe Bridge Street and into a lorry under Fetch's supervision.

'We want you for your muscle, lad,' the bulldog had said encouragingly, pinching his biceps in a flattering way. Outside, a thick-necked lookout man kept watch, hands thrust into the pockets of his raincoat.

When the woman turned up, it seemed to be by arrangement, since Fetch took her into a corner for a brief muttered conversation.

She was still hanging around after the first lorry had driven off, talking in a low voice to Fetch about 'deliveries'. Jarvis couldn't believe that a looker like her was involved in something like this. What was she doing there, getting in the way of men's work? Then he made the mistake of brushing rudely past her once too often.

Fetch observed his sulky reaction calmly. The boy was going to take his punishment and not cut up rough with her, that much was obvious. Ashover had caught him off guard, always the best way to break a rookie in. And there was something about a woman giving a man a belting that turned him back into a scared little boy blubbing in front of his mother. For all his big talk of razors, this one was going to fall into line.

The bulldog had a notion that Jarvis was hiding something. A few drinks might get it out of him, or another smack round the kisser from Ashover, who liked to wear her gloves to protect her nails when doling out punishments. He had seen her hitting a couple of bints in the face before, which he didn't take seriously, but that punch she had given the boy had been a blinder.

'Let's get out of here,' he said softly as the other two men closed up the back of the second lorry and climbed into the cab. He gave Jarvis a wink to assuage his wounded pride before leading the way back to his Roadster, parked further down the road. 'You'll be in charge of carrying bigger cargo next time, Eddie,' he promised Jarvis as he drove off. The kid, as he thought of him, was slumped in the back seat of the car while Ashover sat in the front next to him.

Carrot and stick, carrot and stick. Best to make him feel like a man after that clobbering. Anyway, he was useful. Young enough to be trusted by the gormless, at any rate. Talking of trust, in his experience, you could never completely rely on the really good-looking dolls. They had too much power. They had only to bat their eyelashes to make some fool roll over with his legs in the air.

He glanced sideways at Ashover's profile as he drove them home: Jarvis to the cramped flat above a shop that he shared with his parents and brother and then the matron to Rake Hall.

In some ways, Ashover reminded him of Cissie, who was due to come up to Oxford soon from London to collect the latest consignment from Rake Hall. Classier, of course, and quite a bit more lethal in that cold way of hers.

He had never quite forgiven Cissie for trying to trap his best friend. The slag had paid the price, that was true, and now she made herself useful. But one of these days he was going to teach her a lesson in respect she wouldn't forget.

*

Back in his little house in Cardigan Street, Fetch was brooding over more elaborate plans than mere coal deliveries.

Trading in live exports, as he thought of them, had been his boyhood pal Victor's idea. An extravagantly quiffed, green-eyed charmer, Victor was well placed to know how many illegitimate kids were being born in the town every year, having fathered quite a few of them. 'Surplus stock,' he called them. And as far as shifting livestock was concerned, snoozing babies wrapped in shawls and blankets were a lot less bother than, say, a lorryload of squealing pigs.

It all began during the war when Victor had left Cissie in the lurch. She took it badly, so he quit Oxford and went to ground in London, where he found work as a volunteer firefighter and secret looter after every Luftwaffe raid. Plenty of rich pickings there. 'House clearances' as he called them.

Eventually the stupid mare risked the bombs and pursued Victor to the Smoke. It was obvious to Fetch that he was going to keep on using her, though not in the way she had hoped. Cissie knuckled under – not much else she could do – and proved herself a natural little earner.

When Fetch was demobbed and went back to the old bulldog job at Christ Church that had been left open for him, Victor got in contact to let him know about a thriving bootleg business in London with an Oxford sideline in baby-selling that needed the firm hand of his old mate on the tiller.

You had to be hard to get involved with live exports. Fetch didn't care about kids, and neither did Victor, judging by his track record, so the racket was perfect for them.

Fetch found himself having to liaise with Cissie, although he never completely trusted her. The list of Victor's conquests was a mile long, and Fetch hadn't liked any of them.

Ashover, however, was just the kind of cold fish that the operation needed. In Fetch's opinion, women were usually too emotional, and for a job like this, a maternal instinct was a big handicap. You had to control the blubbing mothers all the time and not lose your nerve.

The matron was about as maternal as his old drill sergeant, who would skewer you as soon as look at you. If she had a secret weakness, Fetch hadn't managed to ferret it out yet.

CHAPTER 22

In a rare outburst one morning as he tidied Lewis's rooms, Squirrel had worked himself up into a real two-and-eight, as he called it, about college bulldogs.

It was time to ask him outright what he thought of them as a breed. Natural enemies, probably – though one could never be sure with Oxford politics.

With the bullers' shifts starting late in the evening and lasting till early in the morning when all law-abiding scouts were tucked up in bed, their work paths rarely crossed. Yet there was always a hierarchy in university circles, and the occasional big-headed buller would sometimes make the mistake of sneering at a scout's domestic duties as vastly inferior to policing student morals – particularly in pubs, where they might consort with women of the town.

Squirrel mentioned an unnamed bulldog from Christ Church who seemed to infuriate him. 'I don't mind telling you that he takes liberties, Mr Lewis, particularly with the undergrads. Lends them money and charges blackguardly rates – he's a real loan-shark. And then there's all the dodgy under-the-counter stuff.

'He's trying to involve Magdalen men now, and it's going to bring the college into disrepute if he carries on like that. He bribes his way through it all and thinks he's untouchable, that he's king of it all. It's gone too far. One of my gentlemen is on his uppers because of this bastard's behaviour – he's even talking about ending it all. Sorry about the language, Mr Lewis.'

The don had widened his eyes at that point, hoping for more revelations if he played the unworldly intellectual. Yet the scout suddenly stopped mid-rant, clammed up and started dragging a duster along Lewis's laden mantelpiece as if he had said too much.

Drink needed to be taken to loosen his tongue, so perhaps he should be invited out to the pub one night – maybe the jazz one, the Perch.

Squirrel's tirade was still at the back of his mind when he decided to embark on long-overdue research into the origins of Rake Hall. Any book mentioning it as a refuge was as likely to be found on the moon itself as in Magdalen's magnificent libraries. The Bodleian was a better bet, however, because of its status as a legal deposit library.

Wearing his spectacles, and with his rather battered hat pulled low over his domed forehead in a way that unwittingly imitated a certain Detective Inspector John Gosling, Lewis headed for the Broad.

Much of his writing was done in the Bod's Duke Humfrey reading rooms, but none of the staff seemed to notice him searching the shelves instead this time. Finally, he located a book on local history that included Rake Hall in the index and sat down at a desk.

Books could not be borrowed from the Bod, but he had always been a quick study. And speed was of the essence, anyway: his first thought had been to make sure that none of the Inklings was there. Tollers, for instance, always enjoyed mooching round the Bod.

It was a strange name, Rake Hall, with its echoes of the stock character of the vile seducer from Victorian melodrama: the devil-may-care rakehell who set about ravishing local maidenhood. The house seemed to have been owned by several generations of a family that had eventually fallen on hard times before handing it over to a charity.

Nevertheless, it clung to its now-dilapidated architectural pretensions, with the turret lending the place the look of a small castle. How fitting that it's now ruled over by that witch, he found himself thinking.

What would the local historian have made of the suspected goings-on at Rake Hall these days? Come to that, what about the present-day governors?

He left by the Catte Street exit and crossed the High to the Bear in Alfred Street, where he had arranged to meet Lucy's father again for a quick pint. It was beginning to become a pleasant habit, though finding time for it was the main problem, what with the never-ending pile of essays to mark and his publisher pressing him for another book idea after the publication of *Miracles* earlier that year.

A smiling Standen had a surprise for him. Sitting next to him on the bench was a tousle-haired young man with a Mediterranean complexion and thick black eyebrows over very blue eyes. There was a take-me-or-leave-me directness about him that made a refreshing change from weaselly academic posturing... the Inklings being an honourable exception.

As the man leant forward to shake hands, Alfred said, 'This is my Irish friend I was telling you about, Mr Lewis: Liam Mitchell. He's staying with us for a few days.'

The Dubliner gave a smile that revealed two startling rows of blackened teeth. Later Alfred told Lewis that Mitchell's widowed mother had suffered from prenatal malnutrition, hence the disastrous state of what Cockney Alfred termed Liam's 'Hampsteads'.

Returning his smile, Lewis said, 'Call me Jack.' Status-conscious Alfred had never taken up Lewis's first-name invitation, but his friend had all the breezy classlessness of the Irish. 'Call me Liam,' he replied, fixing Lewis with a bright blue stare and another calamitously dark grin.

Why, he could be quite good-looking if only he got himself some decent dentures, thought Lewis. But affording them must be the problem.

Far from being overawed in his presence, the irreverent stranger launched into a joke about college dons and Mafia dons that Lewis thought might even bear repeating with the Inklings; unlike some stuffed shirts at Oxford, they had a sense of humour.

As Alfred had hoped, his two friends from different worlds also bonded over literature, with Liam recalling how he had once sat worshipfully at the feet of the writer Brian O'Nolan – Flann O'Brien – in Dublin's McDaid's pub to hear words of wisdom. Alas, all that emerged from O'Nolan's alcohol-fuelled brain-fug was a tip for the 3.30 at Leopardstown.

'Ah, the demon drink,' said a sympathetic Lewis, thinking that this second pint really would have to be his last before he went back to work.

Knowing the don liked to hear news about his homeland, Alfred urged Liam to say more about his campaign against the Magdalene convent laundries.

'What is it you want to know?' said Liam, staring curiously at Lewis. 'You're an Anglican man, I gather. I can tell you about the laundries' dreadful reputation. They're workhouses, they've barely changed since Victorian times.'

The don widened his eyes. 'But I don't understand why these nuns go in for such cruelty when their calling requires them to show compassion.'

'It's because many of them have no true vocation, that's the truth of it,' said the other man with a shrug. 'I've known some good-natured ones, right enough, especially a nun-midwife who had a real calling. But many of them are bitter, angry women because the Church expects a quota from big Irish families to enter holy orders.

'Because they haven't been allowed to marry and have babies of their own like other girls, the nuns take it out on the poor unfortunate women in their so-called care. My mother says that a lot of them are just jilted jennets who haven't managed to get a man to marry them, but then old-fashioned women like my mam tend not to be very kind to their kind.

'Mind you, there was a jilted jennet, was there not, in that recent film I saw in London about a bunch of nuns in the Himalayas?'

'*Black Narcissus*,' said Lewis automatically, once again recalling Warnie's gleeful account of high-altitude hysteria and most unholy, indeed, carnal, thoughts that led to just the kind of confrontation the don dreaded most: at the top of a cliff. Were I ever to be a Sherlock, please never let me be locked in mortal combat with a Moriarty, he thought, over the Reichenbach Falls.

'That's the one,' said Liam, grinning. 'You wouldn't have seen that in Ireland, that's for sure. Don't know why their censors banned it, though. The nuns in it were only Anglo-Catholic, not proper Roman, so no harm was done to the spotless reputation of the Hail Marys.'

'You're not religious yourself, then?' murmured Lewis disingenuously, tempted to introduce this loquacious fellow to Warnie as another film-lover – if it were ever safe to reveal his new associates to his brother.

'No, I am not, as I'm sure you've been told by Alfred. We campaigned against the convent laundries in our paper *Young Ireland* because they're undercutting the commercial ones with their slave labour. It's a bad business all right.'

He paused. 'I'm told you're from Ulster. Magdalene convent laundries exist there too – as well as in England, mainly up north. Did you know that?'

To his embarrassment, Lewis did not.

Giving him another of his searching stares, the young Dubliner said, 'If you want to get rid of someone without actually killing them, there's no better way than locking them away for life in a convent laundry where no questions will ever be asked.

'Mind you, I've heard that in Liverpool the locals sometimes help them escape – but then that place has always been a law unto itself.

'As for the Republic, everyone from the army to the Gaiety Theatre, the Bank of bloody Ireland and even Guinness, for God's sake, sends their dirty linen there to be given a cheap swill by the poor unpaid skivvies. That put me off drinking the black stuff when I found out, I can tell you.

'We also heard the girls get scalded from feeding the bedsheets they've washed into red-hot drying machines like some infernal mangle, but they're not allowed to cry out – pain and suffering are good for the immortal soul. Tempting, then, to test that with drawing pins on the holy sisters' chairs when they sit down for the kind of hearty meal that the girls never get.'

The sarcasm amused Lewis, yet the young man's simmering anger grew.

'It's the families that force the girls into these places if they get pregnant out of wedlock. Some of those babies are the result of rape, even incest, yet these workhouses never punish the men, only the women – which seems to me a monstrous crime when it takes two people to make a baby.'

'Precisely the argument I put to someone recently,' said Lewis, thinking of his first edgy encounter with Ashover.

Liam frowned again, then added in a sardonic change of tone, 'In Ireland, sex is still in its infancy – yet somehow the babies keep on coming. There must be a lot of immaculate conceptions, that's all I can say.'

The joke had lightened the mood like sunshine breaking through a cloud. Fascinated by the natural intellect of a man born with every material disadvantage in life, Lewis decided to stay for one more pint.

It seemed that a childhood of truanting to escape school beatings and seek an education instead in his local Thomas Street library had done wonders for this self-made man. One of his classmates had even been killed by a teacher, who hit him on the head with his favourite weapon of chastisement: the leg of a wooden chair.

'The judge threw the case out, saying that the boy only died because he had a tinker's thin skull, so the teacher was back at his lessons within days.'

Lewis was appalled. He had hated his time at his boarding school in Hertfordshire so much that he thought of it as a kind of Belsen, yet nothing in that regime had compared with the tragic tale of the tinker boy.

Robbie Burns got it right about 'man's inhumanity to man', he thought.

At the back of the pub, a Salvation Army girl with a squeezebox in a holdall slung on straps across her bony back had started to sell *The War Cry* to patrons with a few pennies and farthings to spare.

Lewis looked over at the little figure working her way through the male clientele of the public bar after starting in the saloon, where respectable women were expected to confine themselves. But the girl's Sally Army credentials protected her like a talisman. And although there wasn't much flesh on her, she had the strongest-looking forearms Lewis had ever seen on a woman.

Would it be too fanciful to imagine that a new warrior princess like Britomart from Spenser's *The Faerie Queene* – or Tolkien's Eowyn from *The Lord of the Rings* – might be standing among them?

If only.

CHAPTER 23

Lewis reached The Kilns and opened the sitting-room door, feeling both bold and tranquil from all the ale. He stumbled a little on a worn carpet.

'She's on the warpath, Jack.' Warnie rose sleepily out of the depths of an armchair where he had been drooping over the racing pages.

'Don't trouble yourself on my account,' said Lewis quickly, clearing the inevitable plates away and taking them into the kitchen for a quick sluice. The maids had gone home, which at least spared him their quarrels and complaints, and also the daily woman Miss Griggs, who came in to look after Minto's personal care.

'You've been having a drink,' noted Warnie. 'Good for you. Want to join me in a Scotch?'

'Better not,' said Lewis, raising his eyes meaningfully to the ceiling. 'I'll go and see how she is, then I'll have a bite to eat.'

Up the creaky stairs to Minto, who was whimpering in her bed when he opened the door. 'Where have you been?' she quavered.

And then, surprisingly rapidly for her invalid state, she sat bolt upright. 'I have all these dreams about you,' she said. 'I dream you're in the clutches of some devil woman, that you've been tempted away from me. Tell me it's not true, my darling Jack. Tell me!'

Before he could pacify her, she let out a desolate roar.

'Dear Minto,' he began, 'please calm yourself. I'm just a fusty old don. I don't mix in devil-woman circles.'

Facetiousness was a mistake. She glared at him. 'Are you really sure of that, Jack? Are you always careful of the company you keep?' She leant forward. 'As you know full well, I always have your best interests at heart. I shall be praying for your eternal soul, Jack. And I shall be watching you from afar. I have my spies, you know.'

It seemed an empty threat. Who on earth would act as her loyal informant, given that she always seemed to be falling out with everyone? The irascible Minto was the worst kind of impatient patient, raging at his attempts to nurse her and declaring that her elderly dog Bruce – who spent most of his time flat out and snuffling on the kitchen flagstones – could do better than him.

Settling down in a chair by her bedside, he decided to cheer her up with the music-hall song they both liked, 'Don't Have Any More, Mrs Moore'.

'She's first one in at opening time and last out when they shut . . . If you have any more, Mrs Moore, you'll never get to your street door,' he sang in an undertone so that Warnie wouldn't hear in the kitchen below.

Minto giggled, pleased at the attention. She was exercising the tyranny of the weak, he knew that. And yet, in these strange, whispery times, he felt oddly bound to heed her warning to him.

Alfred was napping by the fire, trying to get a bit of kip before the early evening shift. Some instinct awoke him as his daughter quietly opened the front door. He smiled at her with love in his eyes, but this time she didn't smile back.

He had been thinking it was time to clamber up into their tiny loft, bring down the basket of elderly paper chains and hang them above the mantelpiece in the time-honoured way, though it was going to be a dreary Christmas celebration that year with no relief in sight from all the peacetime privations. Yet every year he cherished those transforming little rituals to mark the change of season.

'How are you getting on with the snooping?' he risked sleepily.

She sat down opposite him. Her silence worried him. They shared everything, or so he thought.

'I've found out about something under the counter,' she began.

Alfred snorted. 'There's been plenty of that at the hostel for a long time. I've heard they do business with one of the bulldogs at Christ Church. No wonder some folks are looking bulkier than they ought to be. Bit of a giveaway, eh, Luce? Bound to make the police suspicious. It's just common sense, but when people get greedy, common sense flies out the window.'

He added sharply, 'Be careful, though, Luce. You don't want to cross this buller, believe you me. I've never liked him, though some say he could charm the birds off the trees. They're the ones you need to watch in my opinion.'

'Is it just black-market stuff that's going on there?'

Alfred looked wary. 'What d'you mean, Luce?'

'Dad, do you ever think about Mum these days?'

'I try not to,' he admitted. 'Why do you ask?'

She hesitated, wondering whether her discovery was best buried. Why open old wounds just for the sake of nursing a festering hatred? But she took out the scalpel nevertheless. 'Dad, I'm trying to remember the exact date when Mum disappeared.'

He told her. And then she mentioned the name she had found in the old ledger entry at Rake Hall: Cissie Standen, his wife and Lucy's mother.

In his heart, he knew that the baby she had been expecting when she left him would not have been his. She had strayed too many times. At his worst moments, he even used to blame himself for her flightiness. She had been restless since the beginning of their relationship – it was he who had broached the subject of marriage.

Everything that happened was his own fault for trying to rescue her from herself. Maybe he had not been a good enough husband; perhaps he was just too dull a dog for her with his placid, domesticated, undemanding ways that he hoped would help her settle down.

He had heard it said that some women preferred bastards: there was a sexual thrill in trying to tame them as well as a competitiveness with other women that were vying for them. He started to weep, first for having been betrayed – and then for the wife who had betrayed him.

'Please, please don't, Dad,' begged Lucy. 'She knew what she was doing.'

Alfred raised reddened eyes to his young daughter. 'I don't think she did really, Luce,' he said. 'That's the damned pity of it all. She thought she was too clever for me – but she wasn't clever enough for the other man.'

CHAPTER 24

Detective Inspector Tooley was a shortish, stout man not easily upstaged by taller juniors. Colleagues around him sometimes joked about the Napoleon Complex. Impressed by DS George's track record on paper as a high-flier at his South London station, he was prepared to give the new recruit the benefit of the doubt here in Oxford.

The station certainly needed some fresh blood. The systematic filching of goods in the little city was getting out of hand, and Tooley's superiors were breathing down his neck about it despite the fact that they – judging by the number of official dinners – didn't seem to be going without.

Must be orders from Whitehall: they had to be seen to be doing something, otherwise it was bad for public morale if ordinary civilians started bellyaching over not getting their fair share because so much was being creamed off. So the toffs were flexing their muscles.

Tooley sighed. That's the hierarchy for you. He reckoned he'd probably be better off with a lot less food on his plate at home, but the wife would keep trying to fatten him up like the Christmas goose whenever she got her hands on a bit extra. Not very good for pursuing villains, although now at least he had this tall thin lad to do the chasing for him.

DS George knocked and entered. Tooley turned a crinkled lizard eye on him, taking in his high colour. The boy was nervous, all right, but presumably that was because he was ambitious; just as long as it wasn't for another reason, such as having something to hide.

'You wanted to see me, guv?'

'Yes, I want a progress report on all the robberies. They're stashing it away like good 'uns, George, and we've got to crack down on it.'

'That's what I wanted to talk to you about. My snout's been coughing.'

'Really?' Tooley cocked an eyebrow. 'I'd almost given up on informants lately; they can get richer pickings on the wrong side of the law. I've told management that a thousand times: we need more funds.'

George paused theatrically, savouring the moment. 'Well, things have gone too far even for my snout, it seems. He's told us about a baby-trafficking business that's being run by some of our low-life friends. It's not enough for them to flog contraband meat and fish, now they're selling living human flesh as well. No-Neck doesn't like it – offends his morals as an ordinary decent criminal, apparently!

'The centre of the operation is a hostel for unmarried mothers that I'm sure you know all about, guv: Rake Hall, hidden away in Clark's Row opposite here. I'm told the baby-selling has been going on for quite a while, as far back as the war. No-Neck should have come forward about it before, I grant you, but now he's got a motive for snitching: there's bad blood between him and the one in charge of it all, who he says is a right nasty piece of work. Turns out he's a neighbour of ours – one of the Christ Church bulldogs.'

'Hidden in plain sight, eh?' said Tooley. Despite himself, he was amused at the sheer audacity.

'This one seems to have his mitts all over a lot of the black-market stuff locally. Probably thinks his college will protect him. But contraband babies are another matter.'

His superior groaned. If there was one thing he hated, it was Oxford office politics, and DS George was new to this particular swirling snake pit. 'Ruddy bullers,' Tooley exclaimed. 'Some of them can be a nightmare, the way they like to make out their private army has got as much clout as the proper coppers. And then they go grizzling to their proctors if one of them gets done on a drunk and disorderly charge, so the proctors get all hoity-toity with us and go over our heads.

'But if we can pin the baby racket on this ringleader, then his college will have to damn well stop yapping and let us handle it. What made your snout fall out with him?'

'His daughter's boyfriend got her in the family way by accident. Of course she had to go into the hostel as soon as she began to show, but her plan was to keep the kid afterwards with the help of her married auntie, who agreed to pass it off as a late baby of her own at the grand old age of 45.

'It happens,' added the young detective. 'Back on my London patch, I knew a family that rallied round in that way in Tooting, so the kid grew up thinking his mother was his sister – until they decided to tell him for his 21st birthday present . . .

'But those Rake Hall bastards took No-Neck's first grandchild away almost as soon as it was born and sold it behind his daughter's back. They reckoned that she'd be too ashamed of having an illegitimate kid to make a fuss about it going missing. That's what they rely on for their nasty little game: the women's silence. Which is why No-Neck has decided to blow the gaff on the baby-sellers. But better late than never, eh?

'Of course they wouldn't have done the dirty on the girl if they'd known about her connections. Goes without saying. No-Neck is hopping mad, but he's decided to keep his powder dry and not say anything until he can let them have it with both barrels by turning King's Evidence. I've also promised him that we'll try to track the kid down, though whether we can get very far, I don't know. One baby seems much like another to me – they all look like Churchill or W. C. Fields.'

He went on to explain how the shortages of adoptable babies in Ireland had created a ready market for importers from England.

'So, it's a circular system, eh?' said Tooley. 'A proper little export–import business. When the girls get pregnant over there, they rush over here to give birth so as not to get banged up for life in some nunnery for their sins. And then the babies get sent back to Ireland. But not the mothers as well, I presume?'

'For their sakes, I hope not. They're known as PFIs in official documents: Pregnant From Ireland. Anyway, the snout has promised to let me know when there's another operation planned.

'We can put out a port alert so we can catch them before they get on the ferry. And we'll contact the Irish Gardaí at the other end too – although perhaps best not to tell them the consignments are bound for convents where the nuns sell them on to rich Yanks without children. Might cause a conflict of loyalty for some of those good Catholic boys, so I'm thinking we should arrest them at this end as soon as possible.'

The concept of any police force at the beck and call of a bunch of nuns was a new one on Tooley.

'So, what I wanted to suggest, guv, is that we infiltrate this lot by starting a Ghost Squad of our men going undercover like they do at Scotland Yard. They're masters of disguise: different hats and caps, reversible coats, workmen's overalls, spectacles with plain glass in the lenses – you name it. Some of them even dress up as women.

'They follow the crims, watch them break into premises and then follow them again till they lead them to their fences. All that's needed is a bit of patience. I'm sure you've heard what a big success it's been at the Yard. Probably get us a bigger budget, too.'

Defensive of his patch to the death, Tooley bristled at the mention of the Yard. 'Undercover?' he mocked. 'Look at you, man! You're as tall as a tree. You'd stand out a mile, especially in all the frilly female gear – you'd look like Charley's Aunt.'

George smiled again, sure of his ground. 'I'm not planning to wear any frocks, guv – I wouldn't be pretty enough. But there's a

Detective Inspector Gosling who's one of the Yard's best operators in the Ghost Squad, and he's as tall as me. Granted, London is a lot bigger, especially his patch, so he's not easily recognised. But I do have one advantage here.'

'And what is that, George?' said Tooley, pursing his lips.

'I'm new. Nobody knows me here yet.'

CHAPTER 25

For some while now, Lucy had suspected she was being followed when she was out on her own.

Neighbours were always watching each other in the hope of tracking down a new source of food, but the local butcher in Walton Street had put the familiar 'No Meat Today' sign outside, and all she was carrying home in her bag that evening was a wizened array of unrationed root vegetables.

Hearing a sound behind her, she wheeled around. Under cover of early darkness, in a badly lit part of the street, a man crossed to the other side. The gaunt, hunched-up shape seemed vaguely familiar, but he wore his cap low over his forehead.

Lucy walked on, glancing back once with narrowed eyes to try to give the impression that she wasn't scared. There was no one there, although her pursuer could have ducked into one of several shop doorways. She wondered whether she should report it to the young detective sergeant that Lewis had mentioned meeting in the High. He had thought him trustworthy, which was good enough for her. On a mad impulse, instead of turning right and into the heart of Jericho, she continued down Walton and headed for St Aldate's.

There, a desk sergeant with the sparsest of hopeful comb-overs, sitting in front of a Highway Code poster emblazoned with the message 'Keep Death Off the Roads', looked malevolently at her.

'What can I do for you, miss?' he said with the special satirical inflection reserved for time-wasters.

Wincing, she blurted out, 'I think I've been followed a lot lately.'

'What's your name, miss?'

She told him, in a voice so small that he craned theatrically to hear it. 'I believe I know who might be doing it, and I'm worried, so I thought I should report it to Detective Sergeant George. Someone told me he's the person to see.'

Barriers up immediately. 'Has this person used violence against you in any way, miss?'

'Not yet. But it's frightening. It seems to be happening so often.'

'Is it a boyfriend? Is this a lovers' tiff? Our detectives can't get involved with that sort of thing, miss.'

'No, he's not. I hardly know him, but he's making a nuisance of himself, and I'm beginning to feel threatened.'

'Nothing to be done about that until a crime has been committed, miss.'

Nettled, she said, 'You mean I've got to wait until he does something violent?' Without meaning to, she had raised her voice in the little reception area.

The double doors behind Comb-Over suddenly opened, and

DS George himself came out from the corridor that led to the CID room. He was heading for a pint in the Bulldog; Parris was out on a job and would join him later. He had heard the loud voice – usually they came from the drunks, female as well as male. Yet the look on this girl's face suggested something more serious. 'I'm DS George. Can I help you?' he said.

Lucy gaped at him. He looked quite young, perhaps only a few years older than herself. Her courage seeped away. Why on earth would the police care two hoots, anyway? She had been a fool even to think of appealing to their chivalry. The only way women could win was to be as hard as men, like her bitch of a mother. She muttered an apology for bothering him and headed for the exit.

'What was all that about, sarge?' said George.

'Just some stuff about being followed. Probably a lovers' tiff. You get them all the time. Girl wants to teach him a lesson by reporting him. They're too free these days, women – it's all the fault of the war, they got given too much responsibility. Then when things go wrong, they grizzle and play the helpless little woman. I'd ban 'em from public life if it were up to me. Tarts are too much trouble.'

'But that one wasn't crying,' George pointed out. 'And she didn't look like a tart to me.'

'If you say so, sir,' said the desk sergeant with the deferential sarcasm due to rank and youth. 'She did ask for you by name, though,' he added grudgingly, covering his back.

George was astonished. As he later joked to Parris over a pint, he hadn't realised that his fame had spread that far in the short time since he'd transferred from London. 'What did she say her name was?' he demanded.

187

Comb-Over sighed at the bother of it all. 'Standen, Lucy Standen. Name rings a bell: I think her old man is a scout next door at Christ Church.'

'Small world,' marvelled George. With his curiosity piqued by the girl's desperate air, he resolved to investigate. After all, there was everything for a new boy like him to discover about the little city, where everyone seemed to be connected to each other via those private networks that outsiders didn't know about.

Outside, Lucy broke into a semi-run, not daring to look back.

CHAPTER 26

Phyllis Brumley smiled benignly at the young woman, one of her more promising new repeat customers. She never asked awkward questions and didn't object to popping round in all weathers, even trudging through snow and ice and happy to have a nice long chat over the haggling. This one was becoming quite the little regular.

'Mind you cook this nice and slow for quite a while in the oven,' she advised, proffering a bloody-looking package in return for Lucy's coins. 'Do you want to speak to Vera?' she added.

Startled that Brumley should even know that they were friendly, Lucy nodded nervously.

'Do Vera good to have a pal to talk to,' said the cook, sounding almost solicitous. 'She gets a bit of a temper up when she's had a few, but she's not a bad kid. I can rely on her. I've got her scouring a few pans at the moment, but I'll send her out soon if you can wait a bit. She can stretch her legs round the garden.' She lowered her voice.

'She hasn't got any family, and her only fun is in the Army – if you can call it fun.'

The clear intention was to keep the drudge sweet. When a weary-looking Vera appeared with a coat slung over her shoulders, she brightened at the sight of her partner-in-crime and pointed to a hip flask in her pocket. The girls mooched companionably around the frozen lawns for a little while as they shared sips.

'Mrs Brumley said you were in the army,' Lucy ventured as Vera tipped her head back for a greedier swig of throat-warmer with the cheery toast, 'Down the hatch.'

'Not the ordinary army. She means the Salvation Army. I'm in the choir. Phyll gives me a bit of time off for that. I'm not a smoker, so I've got quite a strong voice. Friend of mine plays the squeeze-box in the Army's accordion band. She goes round selling *The War Cry* too, but of course I don't have time for all that with the work here.

'I like the Sally Army: they've been good to me since my dad and mum died of TB. They're like a second family. Best not to let them know how much I knock back, though,' she added, grinning. 'They'd all be praying for my salvation. They're strict, but they're kinder than this lot,' she added, jerking her head in the direction of the house. 'You won't get treatment like this from them.'

'What do you mean?'

'I mean,' said Vera, breathing heavily in the cold air as she banged her moth-eaten mittens against her sides to warm herself up, 'that they run their mother-and-baby homes a lot better than Rake Hall. They don't make them go down on their knees scrubbing floors like charladies for a start.

'I got my standards, I have, and sometimes I get really angry about what I see here. Then I tell myself I'm going to do something about it.' She drew closer to Lucy, whispering. 'It's finding the chance, that's the thing. But I'll do it soon, you can bet your life. That screaming is beginning to get on my nerves.'

'Do you mean when they give birth?' asked Lucy, as ever feeling out of her depth when a conversation turned gynaecological.

'No, not that,' said Vera. 'You can expect *that* on and off all the time. It's natural – even if they give them gas – and then the babies start creating as well after they pop out and draw their first breath.

'No, one of the girls has been shut up in the sin bin for misbehaving. That's where they put the ones that cut up rough when their babies get removed. Even though they've agreed to it and signed a bit of paper, sometimes they have second thoughts.

'The off-the-books cases are the worst, of course: the mothers start shrieking and bellowing, imagining a terrible fate like slavery for their kids, and one of them even went for Ashover once. She walloped her back, I can tell you – but only across the face. She wouldn't do anything to endanger the baby: too much money involved to give the mothers a really good hiding.'

Seeing Lucy wince, she added, 'Usually, they knuckle under then and calm down. The sin bin is a padded cell. Ash used to be a psychiatric nurse – the word is that she got struck off for stealing drugs – and she nicked the idea from there. It's an old storeroom that she had lined with horsehair-stuffed canvas to make it soundproof, although of course it's round the corner from the birthing room where people are screaming their heads off anyway. No windows, and there's a spyhole in the door to keep an eye on them.'

She paused, then lowered her voice to a melodramatic whisper. 'This recent one is putting up a real fight. She'd better watch it – she'll get a fist in the face from Ashover at this rate. Ashover is spiteful like that, especially with the pretty ones. She doesn't like competition, and she's stronger than she looks, what with heaving all those barmy patients around in her old job.

'Whenever they have to open the door to go in with this new one's meals and take her bucket away, you can hear her creating something awful and shouting about her rights. That's what my spies tell me; I can't hear all of it if I'm down in the kitchen. Her name's Susan – she gave me a few letters to post, but I don't know any more about her than that.'

There was no moon out that night to show the blood draining from Lucy's face.

'The funny thing is that she hasn't even given birth yet,' Vera mused, frowning. 'Apparently, she's not due for several months, so why she's making such a dust-up now, I don't know. My mate Ber – one of the others told me that Ash reckons this Susan is a troublemaker.

'It's upsetting the others – they're all wondering what's going on – and it'll get the place talked about if the day nurses hear it, which is the last thing Ash, Elsie and Phyll want, obviously. So they're going to move her elsewhere very soon, probably in the next couple of days.'

'Where to?'

'Up north. Something about a Magdalene home in Liverpool. I hear they really crack the whip in those places, so it'll be much worse than here.'

Struggling to stay calm and think clearly, Lucy asked, 'But how will they manage to get her up there if she's causing such a row? She'd scream the place down.'

'You obviously don't go to the pictures that often,' tut-tutted Vera. 'Chloroform plus barbs and sleepers can knock people out good and proper. Then they can be tied up and gagged and chucked into the back of a van. Don't forget that Ashover knows all about drugs.'

Something about the anxious tone of Lucy's questions made Vera look speculatively at her drinking buddy, sizing her up. Though Lucy was not tall, she looked strong and sturdy enough. Vera grinned at her with a hint of devilment. 'You wanna help her escape? We could get her to a better home than this one. My friend Winnie in the Army band would be good in a scrap. She lives very near here.'

'But how would we get her out of the sin bin?'

'Take a look at those holes in the hedge,' said Vera. 'You and Winnie could wait on the other side of it in the street until I give a signal with a whistle to let you in through the kitchen. Might have to be late at night when we can shin upstairs quick without anybody seeing us.

'I reckon I can easily pick that lock too.'

CHAPTER 27

Ashover would rumble him soon. That much was obvious after her hint at blackmail. He kept telling himself he didn't care: his conscience was clear that he had done nothing wrong, he was simply delivering a sympathetic Christian message. Nevertheless there was no getting away from it – his secret association with a house full of fallen women would make malicious tongues set up a bigger clucking than Chaucer's *Parliament of Fowls*.

Despite Dorothy's advice not to go looking for Susan Temple, he had a hunch that the Oxford-born, Oxford-educated daughter of the Reverend Henry Sayers would know all about the existence and purpose of Rake Hall.

A few years ago, Dorothy's liking for a libation or three had resulted in a startling disclosure to Lewis. So far as he knew, he was the only person outside her family who was privy to her own great secret. Even in academe, where writers' reputations could be skewered by the rapier thrust of an allegation, he had never heard the merest whisper about her hidden history.

She was coming up from her Essex home for another Socratic Club lecture several days after his second and almost certainly last visit to Rake Hall, so he suggested another Common Room drink afterwards. He had always felt he could talk to Dorothy like a man. Another stereotype, of course. He had been much amused by her rigorously argued, tongue-in-cheek essay 'Are Women Human?'

His hunch was right: she showed no surprise at the news about Susan.

'Poor girl. Perhaps she hated the regime there so much that she has gone to stay with a trusted friend. Yes, I know about such places, Jack. Call it the secret female grapevine if you will – one to which men are not usually privy unless they absolutely have to know.

'That particular one has been there ever since my father was chaplain at Christ Church Cathedral; he talked about it to my mother once, and she told me, perhaps as a dire warning to a daughter! I must say,' she added, 'the information came in useful eventually.'

Jack stared. Was she hinting that she had been forced to stay there herself? She did not elaborate.

'I would say that it's imperative you don't inform Somerville about her stay there. Best not to burden them with it, otherwise they might feel impelled to use the ultimate sanction and send her down in absentia. She's much more deserving of pity than censure and the problem will be removed in the fullness of time so she may well be able to resume her studies next year without anyone knowing why she had to stay in such a place. Why needlessly rock the boat and risk ruining a girl's future?

'Meanwhile, if she's not close to her parents, as you told me last time, she will be feeling horribly isolated wherever she is now.'

Lewis grimaced. 'The mother seemed to be a posturing show-off, full of herself. I was surprised at how brittle the girl seemed for her age, perhaps because she was always trying to outdo the men. But those of us that loved our mothers don't have that hard shell.'

'A cold mother,' guessed Dorothy. 'So, when Susan grew up, perhaps she mistook sex with men for the love she was missing, as some young women do.'

'I wanted a woman's perspective on this as well as the view of an Old Somervillian. Dorothy, you're a treasure.'

She snorted, brushing off the compliment like dust from her jacket. 'I will say this, though. There's a Somerville scout called Hilda who I've found pretty trustworthy – a matter of me getting much too squiffy at one Gaudy Night reunion dinner and her being decent enough to rescue me from making a fool of myself without saying anything to a soul. She's been there for years, a bit of a college institution, and she's well liked because she's discreet. If you do need to sniff around there at all, choose her.

'Perhaps Somerville needs to be eliminated at any rate, because your girl has obviously gone to ground somewhere. But whether voluntarily or otherwise is the question. Maybe she found out some horrors at Rake Hall, so they've decided to neutralise her.'

He felt a jolt. 'Do you mean killed her?'

'Don't panic, dear Jack – perhaps my imagination is running away with me. There are other ways of keeping people quiet than bumping them off.' A gleam appeared in her beady eyes. 'Wish I'd known about this for one of my plots, although it would probably be too hot even for me. Quite a big scandal for Oxford.'

She gazed affectionately at him. Her fictional hero Lord Peter Wimsey had also suffered from the same shell shock as Lewis in the First World War. Like Wimsey, Jack seemed to be the ideal amateur detective – on paper at least. No one would suspect a high-minded academic of being a secret sleuth, just as people assumed the aristocratic Wimsey to be a chinless wonder without a brain cell. And yet Lewis had always been one of the more down-to-earth dons, even if the arcane thrillers of his Space Trilogy belonged in the realms of other-worldly fantasy.

'A pity,' she teased, 'that you don't care for detective stories. Even mine.'

'Well, saving your presence, I don't as a rule,' he admitted, 'except that I find myself in one. I think I'll take your advice and get Lucy's father to contact this Hilda woman on the scouts' grapevine and ask if she's heard anything of Susan's whereabouts – just in case she's confided in her. Although Lucy said that Susan told Hilda she had glandular fever and had gone home, so we need to find out whether the scout has swallowed that excuse before we go blurting anything out to her.

'At some point, I need to alert the hostel's governors about what's been happening on their premises, but the problem is getting the timing exactly right so as not to foil any police operation.'

Dorothy nodded approvingly. So far, the old boy seemed by happy accident to have all the right instincts for a first-time sleuth. It also struck her that perhaps Jack's entire life of research, dedicated as it was to rigorous academic enquiry, made this don-detective just the right kind of tenacious investigator to root out the truth.

Reassured, he turned the conversation to literary subjects while they drained their drinks. As Dorothy got up to go back to her visitor's room, she said casually, 'My nephew John Anthony is doing very well, by the way. He won a scholarship to Balliol a few years ago, just like my Wimsey; I was so proud of him. Who knows, your student's child may do equally well in time with the right adoptive family, so all is not lost in these situations.'

By vouchsafing this precious extra piece of her personal jigsaw, he realised that she was thanking him for his loyal stewardship of her secret: the birth of a son, brought up by Dorothy's aunt and cousin and passed off as her beloved nephew – in whose education the supposedly childless author took the greatest of interests.

He gave her a clumsy hug before walking drowsily back to his rooms.

Squirrel had turned down the sheets as usual, and all looked comfortably tranquil, just as a don's well-ordered routine should be. He was about to change into his haphazardly patched pyjamas – even someone as cack-handed as him had learned to sew after a fashion during his military service – when the phone rang urgently from his sitting room.

'Mr Lewis, I have to talk to you.'

It was Lucy, calling from a telephone kiosk. The line was a crackling one, and her voice sounded distant. 'I've found out that they have her locked up there, but they're going to move her elsewhere very soon before she squeals.'

No names, just in case someone might be listening in on the line. With Lucy parroting such lingo as 'squeal', Lewis felt as if he had been pitched headfirst into one of Warnie's beloved gangster pictures.

'Can you meet me tomorrow morning at our usual place? I'll tell you more then.'

No peace for the wicked. He lay down to sleep for a restless night of violent dreams.

CHAPTER 28

Instinct told Fetch that it was time to pump the boy good and proper. Over a pint in the Bulldog, he leant in and said, 'Is there something you need to tell me?'

Jarvis looked frightened and then faintly defiant. 'What d'you mean?'

'I mean . . . there's something on your mind. I can tell. I like to know everything that's going on in this town, so spill the beans, son. Maybe I can help.'

He listened as the young clerk described how he had found out about a baffling friendship between a girl at work and a middle-aged man that she kept meeting.

'It's not right,' muttered Jarvis. 'He's much too old for her. It's not decent. Girls need protection from old codgers like him. He goes round to her house at night, and they have tea together in Lyons as well.'

The bulldog didn't bother to ask him why he had been trailing the girl in the first place; it was obvious that Jarvis was driven by jealousy. When would these doll-dizzy fools realise that women weren't worth it?

'Funny thing is,' added Jarvis, 'that they've both been going to this place round the corner from here. Twice now. It's called Rake Hall; that's what it says above the gate. I dunno what it's all about, but he rings the bell at the front door while she goes round the side. She seems to be buying stuff, and then she hangs around in the garden with some girl in an apron, knocking back the booze. She's gone there on her own, too, but I couldn't understand why she went there with this old bloke. She leaves the place before him, and then he comes out later.'

There was a moment or two of silence. Fetch's eyes went navy. 'Is that so,' breathed the bulldog. 'What does this man look like?'

Jarvis shrugged. 'Late forties, maybe. Not much of a sharp dresser. Quite burly but doesn't look like a rozzer to me. I saw him in the Perch when I was doing a gig there; the bloke he was with called him Jack.'

There was one more thing to disclose. Like all informers, he was beginning to get addicted to the feeling of importance. 'I saw the girl go into the police station over the road recently, but she didn't stay long. Scarpered soon after.'

'What's her name?'

'Lucy. Lucy Standen. Her dad is one of the scouts at your college.'

Fetch got to his feet. 'Drink up, lad, look sharp. I need to make some enquiries.'

The youth mooched off obediently into the darkness, smugly

aware of his revelation having hit home and pleased to have got a drink out of it. Fetch made for the nearest telephone kiosk.

'Something you need to know,' he said quietly into the receiver. 'Let's have a pow-wow soon outside your place.'

It was raining again, and a wind was getting up, too. He turned his collar up and pulled his hat down low over his forehead as he headed back home to Jericho. As he reached his door, an exquisitely finished pair of curtains opposite trembled slightly in the draught.

CHAPTER 29

A very unexpected visitor arrived at the Standens' front door. When Alfred opened it, a tall young man produced his ID.

'Sorry to trouble you at home, sir, but do you have a daughter called Lucy?' said DS George, smiling reassuringly. 'A few days ago, a young lady called Lucy Standen came into my police station in some distress. I'm told she had specifically asked for me by name, but in the end she decided not to tell me what the matter was. It left me concerned about her welfare, so I thought I'd see if I could help. A colleague told me her father was a scout at Christ Church, so I looked up your name on the electoral register. I hope you don't mind.'

Wordlessly, Alfred showed him inside and took himself off to the kitchen, trusting to his clever daughter to handle this latest twist. The intent expression of the young law-enforcer in their living room spurred Lucy on to greater confidences as she realised that he was older than his boyish looks had at first suggested. She mentioned her suspicions about a place of so-called refuge, and he gave a start at the name.

'I know about Rake Hall, and I'll tell you more in a minute, but go on with your story, miss,' he said.

Even Alfred's discreet grapevine enquiries via the Somerville scout Hilda hadn't provided any leads about Susan's whereabouts. The college had accepted without question her excuse of glandular fever, though something in Hilda's demeanour told Alfred that she might suspect more. When Lucy told George that Susan's tutor C.S. Lewis had recommended him as someone to turn to for help, the detective whistled.

'Struck me as a steady and reliable type when I bumped into him. I could hardly believe the coincidence: he looks just like one of the inspectors back at the Yard, even though he swore they weren't related. I'm told he's a well-known author, but you wouldn't think he was famous to look at him. Good of him to get involved in your case. Don't worry, miss, we'll rescue your friend.'

George had a tidy mind, if not a tidy exterior, and he liked to tie up loose ends. He was also beginning to speculate about whether the stalking was connected to the Rake Hall case. Given what Lucy had been up to lately, there could well be more to it than just a jealous boy following the girl he was obsessed with around town.

'Do you think your prowler knows you've been meeting up with Mr Lewis and going to the hostel?' he asked.

Lucy felt a cold shock down her spine. 'It's possible. He could have seen us together anywhere and everywhere. Oh gosh, how horrible.'

'Well,' said George, 'let's keep this Eddie Jarvis firmly in our sights as one to watch, shall we? As for Rake Hall, I can tell you now that we've had our eye on it for a while now because of reports from informants about all the illegal activities going on there. We've been planning a raid on the place, but we're going to bring it forward. In fact, it's going to take place tomorrow night – and you can help us, miss. We should be able to get your friend Susan out of there and catch the baby-snatchers at the same time.'

He glanced round the room: no telephone, not that he had expected such a luxury in the modest little two-up two-down. 'If you can be at the kiosk opposite at seven o'clock sharp tomorrow evening, I'll ring you.'

Lucy shivered. Hanging around at night on any street not on a bus route was not recommended for nicely brought-up girls, especially near a telephone box, according to a precocious schoolfriend's mystifying advice. 'Yes, of course,' she said. 'I'll be there.'

He gave her a reassuring wink. 'By the way, give Mr Lewis a bell about the plan as soon as we've spoken. Obviously, I can't give away any operational details, but it would be good to keep him informed that we're going ahead: he could be a valuable witness when it comes to prosecuting Ashover. Will he still be in his rooms at that time of night?'

'He'll be there. In term-times during the week, they all have dinner in Hall at 7.30.'

'Good. I also want to find out if he has any background on the man in the middle of this racket. He's a bulldog at Christ Church; your dad would know about him, too.'

'I doubt it,' she said quickly. 'Dad likes to keep his head below the parapet in case it gets shot off.'

The detective smiled at her defensiveness. 'Your Mr Lewis can sail above all that, can't he? He's got the status, he has. And I'm willing to bet he might have picked up a hint or two, even though it's not his college. Just ask him.'

'Will Ashover get hard labour?' Lucy changed the subject, her wild imaginings trying to picture the matron breaking rocks like Oscar Wilde in Reading Gaol, whose *Ballad* she had read at school.

'They might get her sewing mailbags if they sentence her to penal servitude. Funny how women get off more lightly than the men when it comes to criminality, whereas the men get off more lightly than the women when it comes to morality,' he mused.

'They never give women the Cat like they do the men in a case of robbery with violence. But I don't hold with flogging prisoners anyway: it's sadistic, and it just makes 'em into hardened criminals, in my opinion. What have they got to lose? Anyway, I hear the government is abolishing it next year; that's the word from my guvnor, and about time too.'

He smiled at her, crinkling that snub nose. With his flung-together clothes and his reassuringly open manner, there seemed nothing stand-offish about him. 'Thanks for your cooperation, miss,' he said.

'Call me Lucy,' she said shyly.

CHAPTER 30

The two women in the third-class carriage of the Oxford train from Paddington passed unnoticed by the male gaze, which was not how Cecily – known as Cissie – usually liked it. She relished making an impact. But a job was a job, and she was fly enough to be low-key when she needed to be.

'Gis a fag, Reet,' she murmured to her placid little second-in-command. 'I'm gasping for one last one before we get there. We wouldn't want to harm the little dears' lungs, and of course the nuns wouldn't like it at the other end.'

Rita shot her a warning look as she fumbled in her bag, but the only person within earshot was a fat commuter opposite who was gently slumbering, his bowler hat balanced over his considerable corporation.

Cissie smiled and leant back on the bench, patting her freshly waved ginger curls. She was a calculated risk-taker, the key to her audacious success so far, and all was going like clockwork as usual.

There were no births due at Rake Hall for the next 24 hours, according to the matron – although these things could never be guaranteed, since babies had their own schedule, of course. But if they happened to bump into a midwife or even a doctor coming in and out of the place, Cissie and Rita knew how to be discreet.

In her own way, Cissie was quite solicitous towards her tiny charges and gave them the bottle long before they bawled for it, but she had never had much truck with motherhood. In her opinion, it held women back. She had nearly come a cropper, of course, and the memory of her abandonment still rankled. It was the old story: she thought she was in love with the man, enough to leave her husband, but the bastard had let her down at the last minute.

Victor was almost good-looking enough to be in the movies; she used to tell him that sometimes. But when she fell pregnant, he didn't want to know and promptly decamped to London. The rumour was that he had other girlfriends in the capital, though that didn't stop her following him down there as soon as she could in the hope of rekindling things. But he betrayed her again, just as she had betrayed her husband – what, after all, did she expect?

Fetch was very thick with Victor and none too friendly to her. He and Cissie had always circled each other like wolves, each recognising the other as a natural pack leader. So, there was no love lost, yet someone with her brazen ability to reinvent herself and local knowledge of Oxford was an obvious recruit to Victor and Fetch's little empire. And she had to make money somehow.

Although Fetch disliked her, he had to admit she was a good

team leader. And they needed her more than she needed them: not many people could organise her girls in well-drilled shifts in the way she did. They traipsed up and down from London so many times that they kept wearing out their shoe leather.

Cissie had always suspected the source of that underlying hostility towards her, although, priding herself on being a woman of the world, at first she hadn't seen Fetch as the type. Some people were good at masking their inclinations, though. She had noticed early on how possessive he was about Victor, the ladies' man. *I suppose that's his little secret. He wouldn't like that revealed, oh no.* She smiled again. It was nice to have something on a man like Fetch.

They dragged their small cases down from the overhead rack and alighted on to the wooden platform at Oxford General station, a humdrum disappointment to every starry-eyed freshman that expected to be greeted immediately by a backdrop of dreaming spires. A porter passed by with his oil-lamp. Fetch was waiting for them, giving Cissie his usual sharp once-over; he could ignore the reliably drab Rita.

'Tone it down a bit,' he said menacingly, pointing to her freshly applied red lipstick and the top buttons of her cape coat that she had automatically undone despite the bitter weather and the early darkness of winter.

'When have I ever let you down? Don't I look like a devoted mother?' She smirked, sauntering past him to a parked Austin Ten where Eddie Jarvis was waiting in the front next to a tall youth with a crocodile grin in the driver's seat who answered to the name of Sid. Fetch's precious, much-polished Triumph Roadster was never used for such jobs.

'Not much,' he said, slipping a fiver into her hand. 'A sabre-toothed tiger mother, maybe, that carries her cubs between her jaws. Hope you packed your wellies; it's going to be a stormy night on the Irish Sea, I hear.' He paused and then beckoned her to one side out of earshot of the others. 'This will be the last one for a while, Ciss, so make sure everything goes like clockwork.'

She looked pertly at him, awaiting further details.

'There's been a bit of a development,' he continued, 'over a very rum pair who've been arriving at Rake together, so my spies tell me. He goes in the front door while she nips round the side to have a chat with the cook, who hands over a lot of packages. And then sometimes she goes there alone and hangs around in the garden, drinking with a girl in a kitchen apron who looks like the skivvy.

'The funny thing about this is that I'm told the man's a don at Magdalen, a real Holy Joe who writes books about religion, and she's the daughter of a scout at my college. There's no reason for those two to be keeping company, unless he's a naughtier boy with the ladies than he lets on.'

He moved closer to Cissie until she could smell his sour breath. 'And guess what the girl's name is, Ciss? This is the best bit. Standen. Now how about that for a coincidence?'

Cissie shivered in the raw night air. 'I don't know anything about it, I swear,' she muttered, dazed.

'You'd better not,' he said menacingly. 'But it's all in hand: Ashover is planning to squeeze the truth out of the kid in the apron. You ever seen that big mangle they've got down in their laundry room? You wouldn't want to put your fingers near that. Although she could always take the booze away from her instead,' he added with a low cackle. 'From what I hear, that would be real torture.' Having planted his bomb, he sauntered away.

That would give the bitch something to think about.

He liked to watch them squirm.

Fetch never drove the Rake Hall 'consignments', as he called them, back to the station but always left that job to others, using his shift pattern of night patrols as a college bulldog as the excuse – always wriggling out of things and not getting his hands dirty.

There was no time for Cissie to panic over what he had just said. She slid into the back seat of the Austin alongside Rita. There were not that many cars in circulation just after the war: most people used bikes or buses, especially in a city with so many narrow medieval streets. Yet contraband babies had to be kept out of the public eye.

It was considered crucial to the operation that the two women were always accompanied in the short ride back from Rake Hall to Oxford General by two men in the front as the driver and co-pilot. That meant that at a distance the occupants could pass as genuine couples, with the men waving the women and their babies off on the train.

Cissie sometimes wondered if the regular station porter, a watery-eyed old soul with a bit of a lurch, ever noticed what had become a recognisable rota of women arriving without infants and then departing with some that same evening.

Since she and Rita were a bit too mature to be carrying their own babes in arms, Cissie had a cover story ready if necessary, having laughed over the cunning of it. 'We're from the Universal Aunts Agency, hired for the goodness of our hearts and the quality of our care. Call me Mary Poppins, why don't you?'

CHAPTER 31

Lucy jumped as the kiosk phone shrieked at seven o'clock exactly. Squeezing inside the smelly, windowpaned cubicle that reeked of tobacco and some other indefinable odour, she picked up the greasy receiver for her instructions and then phoned Mr Lewis to let him know about an 'operation at the place' in two hours' time.

The next thing was to race down to Rake Hall and tip off Vera about the police raid, using the excuse of a nocturnal perambulate with her pal over a libation or two. The big question was whether Vera's Sally Army friend Winnie, she of the mighty muscles, could also be roped in to help with Susan's rescue at such extremely short notice.

Vera opened the kitchen door instead of Brumley, whose broad back could be seen fussing away at the stove. Putting her finger to her lips, the scullery maid joined Lucy in the garden.

'Great – a police raid on this place!' she exulted. 'Long

overdue, if you ask me. They'll be busy arresting people, so we can get Susan out of the sin bin ourselves. I'd make a good police-woman, I would. I managed to get word to Winnie; she knows my two-whistle signal, she'll be here soon.' She paused . . . and then electrified Lucy with her next remark.

'Ashover is after me. She cornered me half an hour ago and said she wanted to see me down in the laundry after she's finished super-vising in the birthing room, whenever that is. She wants me to help out with all the washing, which is a bloody liberty – all the girls have to do their turn there, so why drag me into it? I got enough to do in the kitchen, helping old Brumley, not that Ashover would care about that.

'She says she's been keeping watch on the quiet ones – meaning me and Bertha. She's found out that we're matey. Ash doesn't like that – thinks people are ganging up on her, so she wants to have 'em where she can see 'em – never mind all my kitchen duties. You know what she asked me next?'

'No, what?' asked Lucy, fearing to hear the reply.

'Told me to spread out my fingers so she could look at them and see how strong they were,' marvelled Vera, well into her cups by then. 'She said I should beware how I use the big mangle in the laundry room if I wanted to keep working in kitchens. She said she'd teach me a lesson in how to be careful. I just wring my clothes out myself whenever I get round to cleaning 'em, I've never used one of those blooming contraptions.'

Lucy grabbed the other girl by her bony shoulders, staring hard at her. 'Why would she say that to you? Does she suspect anything?'

'I don't know,' grumbled Vera, shaking her off. 'Give over, won't

216

you? She went looking for Bertha after that.'

'Have you said anything about us to Bertha? Does anyone know that we're going to try to rescue Susan?'

'Ashover pinches her black and blue sometimes to make her snitch about what's going on. But most of the time Bertha's a good girl,' slurred Vera. 'She's my only mate in here, I got no one else to talk to.'

Dear God, thought Lucy, I should never have trusted such a mouth-almighty lush to keep her trap shut and not brag about her harebrained scheme to pick the lock of the sin bin and rescue the prisoner of Rake Hall. At this rate, we'll all be forced to play Dare with Ashover's horrible finger-crushing mangle.

'If Bertha blurts out anything, we're for it,' she said through gritted teeth.

'Don't panic, darlin'.' Vera was burping a little. 'I'm a bit tight, I grant you, but I always work best on a full tank. As long as we get this Susan girl out of the sin bin as soon as possible and then run for it, we'll be okay. Go through the holes in the hedge over there and wait in the street till I whistle for you. Winnie will be there soon. She's really good at the rough stuff if it's needed.'

Reluctantly, Lucy crept across the frozen grass to hide beyond the perimeter hedge. She couldn't help turning round once to stare at the lonely little figure of Vera, who was taking another swig before turning back, armed only with Dutch courage, into the darkness of Rake Hall.

CHAPTER 32

Olly Crombie opened the door to his cramped and cluttered Christ Church room, where discarded cigarette butts decorated the hearth rug and unwashed glasses lay in the sink for his scout Alfred to clear up in the morning.

'Oh, it's you,' he said to the young man in the corridor. 'Haven't seen you for a long time. What brings you here?'

'For God's sake, Olly,' Peter Temple puffed indignantly. 'Let's leave aside the fact you owe me a lot, which you've shown no sign of paying back like any decent chap would. I suppose your Bullingdon bills have used it all up. But I wanted to talk to you about something more important.' He leant forward. 'Don't lie to me. Were you the bastard who got my sister into a jam?'

'Don't know what you're talking about.'

'Are you saying that you never . . . ?'

The two men stared at each other. Olly blinked first. 'Didn't know anything about it,' he muttered. 'Susan never said.'

'Well, it's time you did your bit. She needs help. She's sent me a letter, saying she's in a terrible hole.'

Olly looked aghast. 'D'you mean money?' he hedged. 'Problem is, I haven't got any readies at the moment, unless I ask my old man, which is always a problem.'

'Not yet. Although that will come in useful eventually. I'm here to find out what's been happening with Susan, and I want proper help from you in case things get sticky.'

'How was I supposed to know she's expecting?' whined the other man. 'I thought she'd be more careful than that.'

Peter snarled at the casual insult to his sister. 'Nice girls don't come prepared. It's up to the man to take care of that, as if you didn't know. Unless you took advantage of her?'

'I . . . we . . . we'd had a lot of drinks. It only happened once.'

'Every gentleman knows that you never take advantage of a drunken woman. It's just not done,' said Peter scornfully. 'Unless you save your best behaviour for those simpering debs with rich daddies and you think my sister doesn't count. But it's time you put things right.

'I got the impression that Susan hasn't told me everything. She sounded scared in her note, which is not like her, and I need to find out if she's in any kind of danger where she's holed up. So I need your help: can you get a few of the boys together at short notice?'

Olly blinked again, reaching for a cigarette and lighting it with trembling fingers. In truth, he was a sad sight, but even pathetic wretches in denial could play their part.

Lewis had hung on to his old .303 rifle from his Home Guard duties and stored it in a spare wardrobe in his college bedroom, along with his First World War gas mask. Heaven forfend that he should keep them at The Kilns – the maids would have a fit of the vapours if they found them. They were his mementoes from the vanished world that the ghosts occasionally brought back.

He opened the doors and stared at them. Any lead degradation was, he knew, unlikely: the interior of the wardrobe was cool and dark, the perfect storage space. Yet although he had also kept a few bullets as souvenirs, he had no intention of trying to load the chamber and fire the rifle in his usual fumbling fashion.

The painful recoil had left his shoulder badly bruised at first – and anyway he hated the idea of maiming or killing anyone. Yet the brutes against whom Lucy was going into battle might be deterred by the mere sight of it. As for the all-enveloping mask, it was the perfect disguise for anyone who didn't want to be identified as a private detective.

A plan quickly formulated in his mind to hang around as a reassuring – and armed – presence during the police raid on the baby-traffickers. If any passer-by saw his mask and took him for a ghost from the past war, so much the better: it would help to empty the street at that ungodly hour.

To give him the energy for the enterprise, he trusted to his experience as a hearty walker. He had long surprised himself by how much he could accomplish on holiday with Warnie in the Mountains of Mourne, even scrambling up precipitous slopes, though in truth he was always happier on the flat. He never liked to look down.

They had been going there for years since childhood. He wasn't just a sad old don at his desk – he'd travelled in the country of giants. The thought made him brace his shoulders and stand tall. Even Tolkien, who had loved the Brecon Beacons ever since his boyhood holidays on the Llyn Peninsula, couldn't claim the same walking record as Jack and Warnie.

And then Lewis heard the last thing in the world that he was expecting: a knock on the door of his rooms. Apart from the Inklings on Thursday nights, no one ever visited him after dark – and certainly not without an invitation.

Standing outside in the dark corridor was a fierce-browed, curly-haired stranger with the intense look of a young physicist wrestling with the cosmos – which was exactly what he was during term-time. He put a conspiratorial finger to his lips.

'Mr Lewis, I presume. May I come in, sir?' he said in an under-tone, looking cautiously from left to right before crossing the threshold. 'Sorry about the cloak-and-dagger stuff, sir,' continued the apparition, dumping a knapsack and giant scarf on to the floor without ceremony. 'I'm Peter – Susan Temple's brother. She wrote me a letter, telling me what a terrible jam she was in and that you and her friend Lucy were the only ones who could be trusted.

'She went under the radar in some godawful hostel – didn't trust the woman in charge – and she asked if I could bring her some money since hers was running out. My school has only just finished exams, otherwise I would have been here a lot sooner.

'I've asked for leave of absence before the end of term, saying

I've got a sick old aunt who needs my soothing paw on her brow. They swallowed it, but I had to be careful with the timing. I'm new there, so it would give a bad impression to the other masters if I cut and run too early.

'Susan gave me Lucy's address as well as your college rooms, so I thought I'd try you first, sir, as the senior person. She told me the staircase you were on. She insisted I mustn't let Somerville know I'm here: they think she's gone home because of illness. But I can assure you,' he added, grinning, 'home is the last place she would have gone. She doesn't get on with our parents, and if they knew what had happened to her, they'd abso-bloody-lutely read her the Riot Act.

'Not that I approve of that sort of thing myself, sir, don't get me wrong, but since the damage is done, I have to work out how to help poor old Sue so that it doesn't wreck her future. She spoke very admiringly of you, sir, and counted herself lucky to be here – but then she's pretty bright for a girl.'

He looked respectfully at Lewis, taking in the cluttered surroundings as if admiring a Persian emperor's throne room.

There's nothing like the young for being pompous, thought the don. Most of them have no knowledge of the way life can so horribly ambush you – and yet they think they know it all. Had he been like that? Probably. Until his mother died, he'd thought he was God's little gift.

'I've found your sister to be pretty bright for either sex,' he said mildly. 'I don't make a distinction. Indeed, it could be argued that the average female student has to be cleverer than the average male since there are far fewer places available to them. And although

223

I have to admit that I've not been a great advocate for women undergraduates, I admire the fact that Miss Temple is not afraid to be different, which is always the mark of an original mind.'

Peter nodded blandly. His sister had always been contrary, especially with their parents. She argued and fought with her mother in particular, who made it clear she had never wanted a girl and would have preferred a brother for Peter instead. He, secure and complacent in his favoured status, had never had much of an incentive to side with his sister, whom he only saw in the holidays anyway when they broke up from their respective schools.

But there was an old-fashioned gallantry about him nonetheless, especially when he occasionally caught her crying with rage and frustration. When she followed him to university, he had been secretly amazed that their parents agreed to cough up the fees for a girl. Yet even Peter, always slightly more interested in atoms than in human animals, had tumbled to the fact that their glamorous mother preferred his pretty sister to be out of the way.

'How did you get past the porters' gate?' asked the don, curious. 'They wouldn't have let you in without advance warning from me that I was expecting a visitor; we're very well protected here.'

'Over the wall at the back, a quick hop and jump. I've taken Susan rock-climbing in the hols before now – she's not at all bad for a girl. I did some night climbing when I was up at Cambridge – the grip is better there, the Oxford stone is more brittle. Mind you, those Victorian drainpipes are built to last for centuries. I've got a couple of chums in the Oxford Night Climbers – I introduced one of them to Susan.

'I went to see him before I came here. He's the one who got

her into trouble, so it's down to me for being the bloody fool that brought them together. Pardon my French, sir.

'Technically the Climbers is a secret society, a kind of brotherhood of the night because it's so dangerous. But that's part of the fun. Lots bet on it, particularly from the Bullingdon. They can't see an ancient building without taking a running jump at it. I'm told that the Martyrs' Memorial in Magdalen Street is a favourite. I'm sure you must have heard a whisper or two about it, sir.'

Lewis hadn't – and felt a lurch of vertigo at the very idea.

'They put a potty on a pinnacle near the top last year,' added Peter before collecting himself and remembering why he was there in the first place. 'Sorry, sir, I do tend to rattle on. Comes of being a schoolteacher, blethering away to rows and rows of horrible little boys. But how is Susan anyway? I assume she's still in that frightful hostel?'

'The problem is that she's now a prisoner there,' admitted Lewis, wincing at her brother's look of alarm. 'The office manager there told Lucy that she had left suddenly with no forwarding address. For a student as well-organised as Miss Temple, that was highly unlikely. We've now learned that she's been locked up after falling foul of the matron and will be moved to a much worse place very soon, so we have to act fast.

'In fact, it's happening tonight at the same time as a police raid on the place because of criminal goings-on. Lucy has been liaising with a detective on the case, and she's going to try to spring Susan with the help of someone on the inside,' concluded Lewis, feeling flustered at slipping so easily into such jargon.

'My word,' breathed Peter. 'She sounds quite a girl, this Lucy.'

'Not half,' said Lewis, recovering his self-control and thinking that he really must watch that schoolboy slang before his standards nose-dived. 'I must say, your timing is first-rate. Now that you're here, you can be my second-in-command. We're going to mount guard near the hostel in case back-up is needed. Are you up for this?'

Peter rubbed his hands. 'I did a bit of boxing at Cambridge, and I still keep it up. Let me at the bastards. Sorry about the language, sir.'

'Oh, I think we may need more than our fists,' murmured the don. 'Just don't be too alarmed when I put my gas mask on.'

CHAPTER 33

Less than a mile away, the newly inaugurated Oxford chapter of the Ghost Squad had been preparing for its first operation. The toad-necked double agent who went by the name of No-Neck had given DS George the exact timings for that night's batch of babies who were due to be collected and driven back to the station. If they could be caught there and then, it would save a lot of rigmarole and paperwork at the other end with the port authorities and the transport police.

At first, the undercover police operation went as smoothly as pouring milk from a jug. Disguised in overalls, a four-man Ghost Squad armed with a ladder propped up against two metal arms of a lamp post in Brewer Street had been industriously cleaning dust and soot off the glass. The road provided the only vehicular access to Rake Hall.

As usual, its gas had been sparked by the city lamplighters' long poles several hours earlier at dusk, but George was going on the theory that workmen could plausibly fiddle with anything at any time without attracting attention. Passers-by would always assume that something mysteriously technical had gone wrong and take no notice. In this assumption, he was entirely correct.

In fact, the neighbourhood was deserted apart from a tall, flashy-looking female flaunting herself with obvious purpose on the corner of Brewer and St Ebbe's Street, within whose triangle Rake Hall was discreetly tucked away. The area was dotted with little workshops, closed at night, alongside the Brewery Yard and the rows of dilapidated cottages with a historic reputation for having incubated cholera – all of which made it a very useful no-man's-land for an outcasts' hostel. Since the only other access to the place was on foot through the narrow medieval passage of Clark's Row on the south side, the building was very well concealed from the general gaze.

Had there been anyone on Brewer at that hour, they might have been puzzled when the workmen took no notice of the woman at the end of the street, for all her efforts at self-promotion. Not even the dubious tribute of a wolf whistle.

An Austin Ten soon arrived with two men and two women inside. While the men waited in the car, the women knocked at the front entrance of Rake Hall. Curious to see exactly what he was getting himself into with this mysterious new venture, Jarvis craned his neck in the front passenger seat to stare at the hostel.

Despite the darkness, he immediately recognised the female opening the door as the stunner – in more ways than one – who had taken such a swipe at him in the Cowley Road warehouse. Well, whaddya know. Small world.

To give him Dutch courage, Fetch had slipped Jarvis several Bennies before the evening's operation; the kid was new to the baby-snatching game, after all. His RAF contacts had enabled the bulldog to build up a private supply of Benzedrine during the war. In his experience, there was nothing like speed to get his boys going.

Ten minutes later, Cissie and Rita re-emerged from the place with a baby apiece, carefully cocooned in blankets. But as they slipped back into the car, four men surrounded it in a pincer movement. Rita sucked in her breath, horrified, while Cissie glared down at her sleeping pay packet. This had never happened before. First Fetch's ominous revelation and now this. What was going on, and who had betrayed them to the bogies?

They were all about to be arrested for having no legitimate adoption or nannying papers on them, save for an incriminating-looking document from a Galway convent, when one fretful infant, perhaps sensing the tension or just needing the bottle, started to wail. Jarvis and Sid seized their chance to leap out of the car, leaving the women trapped in the back with the babies on their laps. Cissie glared again, this time at a rozzer who smiled back at the pointless defiance. She knew that the police were not allowed to handcuff women (or juveniles for that matter), but, burdened as she was, she could hardly run away.

'Now, you're not going to drop that precious package, are you, missie? Worth a lot of money,' her captor taunted.

The looming shapes of George and Parris blocked the boys' path while the fourth detective blew hard on his whistle for patrol reinforcements from bobbies out on the beat. The sound could be heard more than a mile away and usually deterred most miscreants, except for the most reckless: Bennies boys on speed.

With a venal look on his pimply face, Sid sounded his own piercing summons between two fingers, banking on there being more than a few of the lads in pubs within earshot to leap on their bikes and sort this lot out.

Then the roughhouse started. Jarvis had made good use of his butcher's biceps with a strong right hook when he moved in close to the young detective, but George hit back with a force and agility that unnerved him. In the end, the temptation to use the razor in his back pocket was too much to resist. He lunged at George, his blade slashing at the chest of the detective's overalls, piercing the rough fabric and the vest below and nicking the flesh beneath.

Not expecting such a vicious fightback from a tuppenny-ha'penny hoodlum, George staggered slightly, then, enraged at the nerve of it, he aimed one almighty kick and upended the boy, who sprawled awkwardly on the pavement with the razor falling from his fingers.

'Don't you bloody dare,' said George through ground teeth to the felled Jarvis.

As Jarvis lay, half-dazed on the ground, his heart banging a frantic drum solo against his ribs from amphetamine overload, Sid – always the most slash-happy of Fetch's young ruffians – was lashing out with his blade at DC Parris. Aiming at his well-padded cheekbone, he caught the tip of a wing-mirror ear instead as the detective constable recoiled.

'Do that, wouldya?' he growled, putting the boot in with as much venom as if the youth had murdered his mother. Sid screamed, clutched his vitals and fell clumsily to the ground, the wrap-around grin reversed into an ugly grimace.

Meanwhile, the tall female at the end of Brewer had abandoned her flamboyant antics and materialised at the front door of Rake Hall, leaning heavily on its doorbell and then seizing a bespec-tacled woman in a managerial-looking suit when she tentatively opened the door. Behind her in the hallway hovered a fat party in an apron, looking fearful.

A keen-sighted observer might at that moment have noticed rapid scuttling movements at the back of the house's grounds.

From their vantage point a few hundred yards away in St Aldate's, Lewis and Peter heard the police whistle. The don whis-tled back, followed by a louder Peter.

'Down the alley,' shouted the gas-masked Lewis, brandishing his rifle as he led the way across the road to the winding Clark's Row.

But someone else had also heard the cacophony of whistles.

CHAPTER 34

This was her third day in the padded cupboard with nothing but a bucket and a small truckle bed at her disposal. Susan's only hope of help – the day nurses on their lightning visits that left scorch marks on the carpet, or so the sour Rake Hall joke went – clearly knew nothing of her captivity.

Within her, a life was stirring, and tiny flickering movements made themselves felt. She had begun to clasp her stomach, savouring the novel experience of a little being within her. She hadn't felt this tender since carefully rescuing a pinioned mouse from a trap at the age of eight, only for the poor thing to die of fright.

Ashover had wasted no time in telling her that she was being moved on very soon. 'It's a former workhouse, not the kind of thing you've been used to, Temple, with your college education and your lah-di-dah voice. That should knock the corners off a hoity-toity little madam like you. With any luck you'll end up a lifer there, and all the better for your immortal soul. This is Liberty Hall by comparison. You should have been a damn sight more grateful.'

She drew close, hissing. Trembling, Susan stood her ground until the matron was finally forced to retreat, wary of damaging the goods.

That temper of Ashover's is a definite weakness, she thought. She wondered why the woman got so emotional. Yet it was hard to keep up the defiance in the face of such personal animosity. She was beginning to lose heart, hoarse from shouting a protest every time the door was edged slightly open to slide in a grudging tray of food. And when were they going to take the horrid bucket away?

Then she heard an unexpected noise that suggested someone was scratching purposefully at the keyhole to her padded cell. Maybe they were changing the lock, just to thwart her still further in case she had managed to take an impression with a bar of soap (as she had once seen in a thriller at the pictures). She hadn't worked out how she would then get a copy made from the impression while still shut up in this hellhole, but by this stage she was becoming incapable of logical thought.

Suddenly her prison door was pushed open as Lucy Standen and that funny little scullery slattern who had posted her letters, together with a girl she didn't recognise, came crowding into her tiny space.

The three-girl cavalry rushed Susan along the dimly lit corridor towards the narrow back staircase, hoping that all the noise coming from the front would help their getaway. Following the great siren calls of competing whistles, fierce yells could now be heard outside the hostel as battle commenced.

'And where do you think you lot are going?'

Cynthia appeared out of the gloom, hand on hip in her usual challenging way.

'Cyn,' breathed Susan. 'So glad to see you. They've had me shut up for days.'

'Yeah, you were a naughty girl – still are, I see. Who are these other two with Vera? Are they running away from the police? The coppers are outside – they've taken Phyll Brumley and Elsie away. Anyone would think they've been breaking the law.'

'Why didn't you rescue me?'

'Are you kidding? And forgo my baby bonus?' Susan's look of horror made Cyn relent enough for a characteristic smirk. 'Now the coppers are here, I don't see much chance of that anyway. Maybe I should ask for an informer's reward instead?'

That survivor's ability to switch sides had to be admired; she really was the perfect double agent.

Susan was about to smile with relief and say a quick goodbye when a malevolent vision in beautiful white fur loomed up behind the grinning Cyn as if it had all been orchestrated. Were they in on this together?

Even as her little empire was collapsing around her, it seemed the matron could still find time to be enraged by the sight of an escapee. Clenching and unclenching her fists, she made a rush at Susan, only to be met instead by Winnie's squeezebox fingers round her slender neck. With the air almost choked out of her, the lipsticked mouth fell open to reveal two upper canines whose strangely feral look did nothing for her beauty and which explained the always tight, self-conscious smile.

The girls agreed afterwards that they hadn't seen such impressive fangs since a wartime outing for Lon Chaney Jr.'s *Son of Dracula* had led to queues round the block. One could almost feel sorry for her.

Lashing out with her heels at Winnie's bony shins, Ashover finally wrenched herself free, almost toppling over in the effort, then clattered down the back staircase to disappear into the gloom beyond.

The four girls followed more cautiously down the narrow steps, intent not on pursuit but on getting Susan to a safe place and away from the mayhem among the men at the front.

A Black Maria had arrived to pick up the arrested women and babies while the pitched battle was still going on. Sid's whistle had brought youthful reinforcements led by Fetch's second-favourite bruiser Sandy, all high on Bennies and spoiling for a fight as more police started arriving.

A few nearby cottage-dwellers dared to peek out, but no one was rash enough to put their lights on. It was as if the wartime blackout had temporarily returned, when everyone knew about, and dared not interfere with, the various dreadful things that could be done under cover of darkness.

Taking advantage of the circling menace between razor and truncheon that seemed to be developing into a dangerous kind of dance, the dazed Jarvis crawled on hands and knees out of the melee. One of the police ghosts had just put another youth in a hammerlock-and-bar hold, deftly twisting his arm behind his back to make him drop his weapon.

In the near distance, Jarvis saw Fetch, who had heard all the whistles during his bulldog patrol and come to investigate – unlike his more prudent fellow bullers, who never ventured next, nigh or near any town trouble whenever police whistles sounded.

Not that Fetch took unnecessary risks, always leaving the more obvious stuff to his fired-up boys who seemed to enjoy flashing the blades around in their youthful squabbles as soon as they started shaving. Taking on coppers, however, was another matter. At this rate, they would all be Borstal-bound.

He turned tail, heading north for Oxford's plentiful back alleys. Revenge was a dish that the fastidious Fetch enjoyed serving stone cold with a side plate of ice.

Behind Jarvis, a weirdly gas-masked apparition from another age had just appeared. It brought its rifle down on Sandy's back just as the latter's blade was being provocatively waved in front of a copper's face. A young tousle-haired man was alongside the gas-masked one, his fists flying in every direction.

Out of the corner of his eye, George saw Jarvis staggering after the fleeing Fetch.

'Get 'im,' he bellowed.

CHAPTER 35

'Does that hurt?'

'Nah,' swanked Parris. 'Pussycat scratch, although I won't be able to wear earrings if we dress up as women next time. Still, never mind, I hear Jonesey enjoyed putting on the frock so much he's volunteered for Ghost Squad shifts all next year. Must be the am-dram he does in his spare time.'

'Or something,' said George, grinning. They were in the Gents at the St Aldate's nick, staring at their cuts and bruises in the mirrors over the sinks. Good to have something besides arrests to show for the first operation of the Oxford chapter of the Ghost Squad. Made them look like heroes.

One of the only two WPCs in the Oxford City Police at that time was looking after the babies, warming up the bottled milk and cooing into their shawls, while interviews with the suspects were taking place. Faced with the prospect of gaol, Cissie had decided to do the decent thing and rat on Fetch. It was not as if she owed him anything, apart from a living that she could make elsewhere.

'I know all about him, darling,' said George. 'I've sent a few men after him. We'll catch him, don't you worry. So, you're an innocent victim of a wicked trafficker, are you?'

Unfortunately, he was flirt-proof, and Cissie was not one to simper in vain. She stayed sullenly quiet after that while Rita huffed and puffed in the next room.

Further along the corridor, Phyllis Brumley was singing like a canary, secure in the knowledge that her co-conspirator Jane Ashover seemed to have disappeared in a puff of air.

Elsie and her corset had also been taken into custody, but she was a deep one. Despite the unearthing of the ledger hidden in the locked drawer, DS George had not yet been able to conclusively prove her role in the baby-trafficking.

At every question, she plaintively repeated, 'That's not my hand-writing. That's Miss Ashover's business. She asked me to keep the key safe, but I don't know why. I wasn't privy to that. I was involved in legitimate adoptions, which all complied with proper council guidelines. You only have to look at my ledger in my handwriting on the desk in my office to see proof of that.'

By her side, a weary-looking duty solicitor on the night shift nodded wan approval of her defence.

Still, at least the police hunt had captured two examples of prize game in Cissie and Rita, caught with the living evidence in their hands. George stared at the ID cards in his hands. He shared the same cynical view of the cards as the Tory MP William Morrison, who had been raging in Parliament only the other day about how the average spiv could boast to having half-a-dozen of them – so what price their value in fighting crime? They didn't even carry photographs.

Luckily, however, Cissie had never bothered to acquire more than one. In her experience, women were rarely stopped by the police – except for the tarts, of course, on a daily basis. But that was their fault for sinking so low. There was plenty of money to be made without selling yourself so cheap.

'So, you're both from London, are you? We'll need to turn you over to the Met. We've got no cells in Oxford for women anyway. I'll get you your own special police chauffeur to drive you back to the Smoke tonight, you lucky ladies, once I've put in a few calls.' He paused, lingering over the names, and looked again at Cissie. 'Standen, eh? Now, where have I heard that before? Any relation to Alfred and Lucy Standen of this parish?'

He had seen a reaction like hers before when an inspired guess hits home: a kind of fury, followed by an implacable, folded-lip stubbornness that people who have turned their backs on their old life draw round themselves like an iron cloak.

'No,' she said.

George let it drop, though he resolved to mention the coincidence of the name to Lucy just to see if any loose ends needed to be tied up.

*

All the while, staggering slightly, the still-winded Jarvis ran through the night streets. At one point the fleeing figure of Fetch in front of him seemed to hesitate before veering off to the left towards Jericho instead of going right towards the High and the Chequers pub, as Jarvis had expected.

The only sound he could hear was his own laboured breathing, the noise of the battle having receded into the distance. The police had probably collared everyone by then anyway, what with the St Aldate's cop shop being so near. The bulldog seemed his only hope of escaping the rozzers. Surely Fetch with all his experience would know what to do.

Glimpsing his quarry ahead, Jarvis slowed down to muffle his footsteps as he passed the opulent basilica of the bulbous St Barnabas before turning into Cardigan Street.

'What in hell's name are you doing here, boy? Has anyone followed you?' In the doorway, with a dim light behind him, the silvery-blue eyes flashed a keep-out warning.

A pause, then Fetch seemed to relent after leaning forward to look both ways along Cardigan. 'OK, chum, you might as well come in now you're here. Get in quick.'

A muddle of rickety-looking furniture was inside the dimly lit parlour. Whatever Fetch spent his ill-gotten gains on, it wasn't home comforts.

'Wait here,' commanded the bulldog and disappeared into the back room. He came back with an Enfield revolver tucked into his waistband, concealed by his jacket. 'I haven't got a spare one here, but there are more in my other place on the High. We're going to need them.'

'I don't know how to use a gun.'

The bulldog looked contemptuous at the objection. 'You'll learn.'

He locked up quickly, again checking the street in both

directions. Neighbouring curtains were all drawn, and no one was around, apart from a skulking cat that shrank away, big-eyed.

With Fetch leading the way, they hurried up to Walton Street, headed south-east along St Giles and then turned left on the Broad before making for the High. Though the noise from the battle had faded by now, Fetch knew that patrol cars could be lying in wait like basking sharks at various points to catch any gang members that hadn't managed to go to ground.

The two of them were lucky, however. They reached the Chequers, which, like all the other pubs in the area, had closed early at the first sound of mayhem on the streets. No licensees wanted trouble on their doorstep, especially if the police were involved.

At the end of the narrow passageway leading to the pub was a doorway to the cellars, which Fetch unlocked. Jarvis followed the gangmaster down the stone steps. Fetch nodded towards a large hole in the wall, beyond which piles of goods had been hidden by his young henchmen to take advantage of the cool conditions.

Alongside them was a veritable armoury: rifles, semi-automatic Sten guns, pistols, some blast grenades, a rusty old bayonet or two stacked in the corner. Even Jarvis realised that most of the weapons must have come from army supplies, stashed away since the war with the connivance of a landlord or pub cellar men in on the racket.

Fetch was a pragmatic man, and it was not his intention to stage Custer's Last Stand with this mini-arsenal. Having realised that the game was up in Oxford, his only thought was to get away. No point hanging around now they'd been rumbled. But if weapons had to be used on the way out, he was going to be prepared.

'That passage leads to more cellars underneath the Mitre oppo-site, though you have to crouch down a bit to get through the tunnel – people must have been midgets in the old days. I don't have a key to get out of the Mitre, so we'd have no exit at that end if it's been locked. If they tracked us down here, we'd be cornered, so we'd have to make a break for it. Never mind, I've got another plan. Arm yourself with that Enfield over there, Eddie. I'll show you how to fire it if you have to.'

CHAPTER 36

At Alfred and Lucy's place, Susan was plied with tea and sandwiches and the least-worst wing-back armchair so that she could rest in front of the fire.

Lucy brought in the old wartime blackout curtains from the Anderson shelter in the yard to add to the threadbare drapes that barely covered the downstairs windows. The less light to be seen from the outside the better, and decent fabric was always in short supply.

Winnie continued to be appalled at all the details relayed by Lucy, who couldn't resist mentioning her part in the police investigation after she had reported her stalker.

'I've seen that Eddie Jarvis before. He plays the drums in a local band, and they always do a namecheck at the end when they take a bow. What a disgraceful fella. Fancy bothering women like that,' she tut-tutted.

'Jazz?' Susan lifted an eyebrow. 'Does the Army approve?'

'You'd be surprised about some of the secret lives in the Army,' said the squeezebox siren demurely. 'Don't judge, miss. Anyway, it's all music, isn't it?'

Lucy was squatting on Alfred's sadly moth-eaten hearthrug, close to Susan. 'What are you going to do?' she asked her tentatively.

'Get it adopted in the official regulated way so I can go back to Somerville with no one there any the wiser. Not that I'll ever be allowed to know the identity of the adopters. But I'd like to think that some day I could find out what has happened to it,' she added, lifting her chin again in the familiar way.

'Maybe it will turn out to be clever like you and get a place at Oxford,' said Lucy.

The remark, intended to comfort, only wrenched a grimace out of the other girl. 'I just hope it will have a happy life. A girl I knew at boarding school hated her adoptive parents. The mother used to hit her with a leather strap for the silliest, tiniest things. But because she was privately educated and given piano lessons and all that stuff, everyone had this crazy idea that they were ideal parents. It was all show.'

Despite Vera's and Winnie's attempts at persuading Susan to move to the less spartan surroundings of a nearby Salvation Army mother-and-baby home, she had point-blank refused. To their consternation, she had decided to return to Rake Hall as soon as possible.

Lucy couldn't believe it after all that had happened. 'Why, for heaven's sake?'

'That's the point, don't you see? The place will be better run now after the governors find out from the police what's been going on. And I suppose I want to see how Bertha and some of the others are. They must have been terrified by the police raid. But I won't be staying there for much longer. I have to move on to another hostel because I'll have reached the three-month limit of a stay there soon. There'll be no more bending of the rules like Ashover did.

'I've got a friend in North London, and she knows about a place in Hampstead, so I'll get a doctor's referral. It's run by the London County Council, so with any luck, they won't make us get down on our knees and pray twice a day like the religious ones do. I've had a basinful of that for one lifetime.

'I'm going to get myself a wedding ring to hide my "shame",' she added with an irony that made Lucy wince. 'I can't get one from a jeweller; they would think it strange if a single woman turned up asking for one and might even refuse me, so I've decided I'm going to go to the antiques stall in the Covered Market. They never ask any questions there. No idea where they get their supplies from, but it's all to the good in my case.'

She looked down at Lucy, who was shivering with what might have been the sudden chill after Alfred's little fire had gone out. 'Don't worry, kid, I'll keep in touch,' she said. 'I'll make sure to let you know my forwarding address – just in case.'

CHAPTER 37

Fetch's boys Sid and Sandy had spilt a whole tin of beans to avoid a GBH charge. The police hunt for the mastermind Fetch was now centred on the Chequers.

When a perspiring Jack Lewis and Peter Temple arrived at the police station in St Aldate's, they found that the reinforcements arranged earlier by Peter had turned up as instructed. It was widely known, though never officially reported, that the secret society known as the Night Climbers of Oxford had quietly distinguished itself during the war by lending its expertise to undergraduates' fire-watching vigils on college roofs in anticipation of the Luftwaffe's incendiary bombs.

Privately, Lewis marvelled at the military-like operation organised by the young prep-school master in the hope of catching his sister's captors. One of the Climbers, the chain-smoking Olly Crombie, looked a rather poor, heavy-breathing specimen to

Lewis's eyes. But at least he had several brawny student hearties in tow to make up for it: college oarsmen, probably, judging by their impressive muscle mass.

'I'll take charge of your rifle, sir, if you don't mind,' said George to Lewis, who thankfully surrendered it. 'Can't risk it going off in a civilian's hands.' He strapped it behind his back with Lewis's belt.

With George and Parris leading the charge, and the student volunteers at the rear, it was a very mixed scratch squad that headed for the Chequers. After posting two of the beefier undergraduates outside in the street as lookouts, George and his little unit pushed open the unlocked door to the cellars and clattered downwards.

To the young men, it was a subterranean adventure, but to Lewis, it transported him back to the deep, waterlogged dugouts of the First World War.

At least this one smells dry, he thought as he took in the cave-like scene, lit by a lone electric bulb to illuminate its hoard of contraband goods. The birds had flown. But where do birds fly? thought Lewis rhetorically.

He lifted his eyes skywards just as George had the very same thought.

'Parris, take two down that tunnel. It leads across the road to the Mitre cellars, so check if they're holed up there. The rest of you, up on the roof. There's a fire escape at the back.'

A puffing Lewis, his gas mask slung over one shoulder, followed George, Peter and two hearties upwards. Somehow it seemed to be his destiny in this strange adventure to attempt what he had never done – or ever dreamt of doing – before. He had taken the precaution of tying his scarf around his face to shield himself from the cold night air and recognition.

The fire escape at the top of the three-storeyed inn ended outside a window below a pitched roof whose summit looked to be just within the grasp of a determined Night Climber. George, Peter and the hearties managed the ascent easily. Below, Lewis waited anxiously. Squeezing past the don with muttered apologies, Olly clambered after the others and squatted athwart the roof ridge that ran along the top of the terrace formed by the Chequers and its neighbouring buildings.

Lewis was hoping and praying that he could stay skulking on the fire escape as another lookout man. No such luck: the altitude had transformed Olly into another creature altogether. He reached down to grab the don's hand, hauling Lewis and his gas mask up with the help of a hearty.

Copying the others in front of him, Lewis sat astride the ridge with its crumbling mortar and then tried to propel himself along by using his arms like oars. He had once seen a legless beggar, a veteran of the Somme, scuttling with surprising crab-like speed along the pavement. Yet such mobility eluded him, his only oarsman experience confined to punting inexpertly across The Kilns' stone-quarry pool when no one else was looking and laughing.

Some of the tiles beneath his feet were broken, and one or two even shifted beneath his weight, the nails that had long ago fixed them in place probably rusty by now. The old sick feeling of vertigo, the world spinning in a circle round him, threatened to topple him from his perch.

In desperation, he summoned all his self-control. But even as the images wavered, he could see it all in his mind's eye anyway. Westward was St Aldate's, the top of the City Chambers, the Electra Cinema and Christ Church, with Corpus Christi and Merton beyond it, all now shrouded in darkness. Behind him was his own Magdalen. Below him on the left was Oriel, the Examination School and University College.

Brasenose was to his right, along with Lincoln, All Souls and Queen's, with the beautiful spire of St Mary the Virgin in between. In the adjoining St Mary's Passage, Lewis had long admired the gilded fauns decorating the porch of a 17th-century timber-framed house.

The single lamp post further along that little thoroughfare always reminded him of the ones that stood sentinel on a stretch of lawn outside his favourite London church of St Jude on the Hill in Hampstead Garden Suburb, where he had twice preached during the war.

He knew every stone of it all, not needing to see what he loved. Fog had descended over the city, partially hiding the moon, and thickened into sulphurous smog by the smoke from myriad household fires as the night grew even colder. The dull light from street gas lamps could barely be glimpsed from where he was squatting.

Through the miasma, on the ridge right in front of him, he suddenly saw a sight he did not expect: a row of silhouettes from his First World War squad, Paddy the last of them. If he reached forward, he could almost touch his lost friend's shoulder.

'Hello, old chum,' he muttered, the sharp salt pang of tears behind his eyes. 'Have you come back to me at long last?'

There was no answer.

He blinked hard to stop the shameful weeping. The figures of the soldiers seemed to tremble and then vanish, replaced by the hunched backs of George's scratch squad as they inched towards their quarry. In utter anguish, Lewis stared starwards, seeking inspiration.

What were the words to that stirring old Unitarian hymn 'Nearer, My God, to Thee'? He recited them slowly to himself, relishing the heartfelt plainness of the lyric about the story of Jacob from the Book of Genesis: 'Though like the wanderer, the sun gone down, / Darkness be over me, my rest a stone / Yet in my dreams I'd be nearer, my God, to Thee.'

No handy Jacob's ladder up to heaven had appeared at his command, yet somehow the comforting thought of seeming nearer to the divine power at that icy altitude helped to calm him a little as he concentrated on balancing. As snowflakes began to fall, the ridge was becoming wet and slippery under his frozen hands. It felt like being at the very top of a fairground Ferris wheel, one of his more daunting childhood memories.

Typically, his next thought was that an even more foolproof way of getting nearer to God would be to lose his footing and fall off.

George's tactic of taking his men to the rooftops had paid off. They glimpsed two figures ahead who seemed to be having as much difficulty hauling themselves along the rooftop as did their pursuers. The one nearer to them, perhaps some ten yards away, had halted bat-like on his perch, looking like a spent force. Not so the one in front of him, however. He looked around and fired a pistol menacingly into the air as a clear warning to the pursuers.

You would always swing for murder, especially that of a policeman, so Lewis guessed that the fugitives were unlikely to shoot to kill despite the first man's threatening gesture. But what on earth was George intending to do in retaliation? Good Lord, thought the don, I would hate my old blunderbuss to be the death of anyone.

Then, the man nearer to them fell awkwardly across the ridge, panting. Seizing his chance, George edged up to him, quickly slid the rifle off his shoulder and brought it across the man's cringing back just as Lewis had done in the battle outside Rake Hall, though the blow was not a vengeful one – more of a sharp tap to establish mastery. It was vital, after all, not to make him – or, indeed, George himself – lose balance. The detective held him down almost protectively, pinning him to the ridge tiles.

The other fugitive levelled his pistol at the little squad riding the ridge and carefully aimed it just above their heads, so close that Peter could have sworn he felt the bullet whistling through the upstanding tangles of his unruly hair. That was when they realised the diabolical intention was not to hit them but to frighten them into toppling off their perch to the faraway street below. That way, no one could finger the gunman for their certain deaths.

Shuddering at the malice behind the manoeuvre, Lewis finally found his voice. 'Steady, lads, steady! Hold the line.' Like a carved column of stone medieval saints with their arms round the one in front on their way to heaven, they clung to each other.

No more bullets followed. Madly redoubling his efforts at self-propulsion, the man disappeared from sight beyond a large chimney stack and into the dark horizon.

CHAPTER 38

The comedown from the amphetamines was a grim and brutal one. Bennies were great for staying alert and combating fatigue, but the tiredness, depression and agitation that followed were accurately nicknamed the vortex of doom. The rumour was that old Adolf himself had been on daily injections of opiates and cocaine – and it was well known that an army could march on its methamphetamines.

But Jarvis wasn't a soldier, drug-hardened and battle-hardened. Up on the roof, he felt horribly detached from his body as if his soul were floating in outer space. The energy was evaporating; he could fight no longer. When the blow across his back came, he curled into a foetal position that was easily transportable. Careful not to lose their balance on the ridge, the Night Climbers lifted him above their heads and passed him to each other along the row like a precious parcel.

At St Aldate's station, he slumped across a chair in the interview room. George knew he wouldn't be able to get any sense out of him until early the next morning when he could be usefully fortified with canteen tea and sandwiches.

At first, Jarvis was inclined to keep his counsel, until the name of Jane Ashover was mentioned. Remembering the humiliation of her blow across his face, he told all he knew of the witch's collaboration with his mentor.

Although many of the gang had been rounded up, the hunt for Fetchley and Ashover remained ongoing. George guessed that the vanished bulldog had slithered down a drainpipe at the back of the buildings along the High and that he and Ashover would head for London or Birmingham, both cities big enough to swallow them up.

Enquiries were made with the Christ Church proctors about the disappearance of one of their bulldogs, wanted for questioning in connection with a nasty case of baby-trafficking and black marketeering. The proctors' shock, followed by indignant bluster at police interference – they would investigate their own, thank you very much – sent Detective Inspector Tooley into such a state of exultation that he treated the newly formed Ghost Squad to celebration drinks, an unheard-of extravagance from him.

A 48-hour watch was placed on the railway and bus stations for anyone answering the missing pair's descriptions. Fetch could drive, whereas Ashover could not, according to Elsie, who had decided to be less sphinx-like and more cooperative as the hours ticked by. There remained the possibility that she had managed to hitch a ride with Fetch, though Jarvis took gleeful pleasure in suggesting that there seemed to be no love lost between the pair.

258

The only trace of Ashover that had been found was an Arctic fox fur coat lying on the grass at the back of the Rake Hall garden, for all the world as if a snake had shed its skin and left it behind. Vera and others, including Lewis, were able to confirm that it had belonged to Jane Ashover.

'She'll be ever so cold without it,' gloated the scullery maid, rubbing her calloused and chilblained hands together.

'We'll track her down in the end,' George reassured Lucy. 'It'll be worth paying a visit to some fancy London dentist in Harley Street. They're the only ones who could file down those telltale dagger teeth of hers you were telling me about – and they always take before-and-after photos for their records.'

As for Fetch, a seamstress who lived opposite him in Cardigan Street admitted to a door-knocking DC Parris that she had glimpsed a bit of coming and going on the night of the raid but thought nothing of it. And no, she didn't know Mr Fetchley to speak to. He was a bachelor gentleman who kept himself to himself and always seemed very busy with his work at the college.

Ethel was damned if she was going to say too much. The police's city-wide search was proving very bad for her fabric supply, that was for sure.

When pressed by Parris, who was convinced such a near neighbour must know more than she pretended, she did concede that the gentleman might be the owner of a Triumph Roadster kept at a nearby garage. Not that she had particularly taken too much notice of the make or model, you understand, but as Parris's interrogation continued inside her little domain, where bolts of illicit fabric were concealed in an old ottoman, she suddenly found that she was able to describe its shape well enough so that the detective could be on his way.

After he had gone, Gladys opposite risked reputational contagion to nip over the road and let slip – head cocked artfully to one side and eyes gleaming – that their neighbour Fetch was wanted for baby-smuggling. Ethel pursed her lips in reflex disapproval.

She tried not to dwell on what he might have done to her if he'd ever discovered her little 'sideline' threatening his livestock supplies.

*

A few days later, DS George dropped in on Lucy to keep her up to date with the details of the investigation and share a cuppa by the fire. To help out, he brought along several pinches of the station canteen's tea-leaf rations in a twist of paper. Christmas was now less than a month away, and householders had begun hanging up homely window decorations. Having a sentimental weakness for the season despite – or perhaps because of – being a bachelor with no family nearby, George was rather touched by the sight.

As he did every year, Alfred had taken Lucy's old tinplate toys from the small loft and put them on display. 'Her mother bought some of those for her, and I've kept them ever since,' he whispered to the young detective while his daughter was brewing up in the scullery.

DS George could no longer delay mentioning the arrest and questioning of the woman who shared Alfred's name. The scout bent his head down as he listened. Then there was a short silence.

'She was my wife,' he said thickly. 'She still is, but we haven't heard from her for a long, long time. Now we know why.'

Neither man noticed that Lucy had crept in from the scullery after overhearing most of their muttered conversation. Alfred looked up and saw something he had never expected: his tomboy daughter's eyes suddenly bright with tears. Not for Cissie herself – she was determined never to cry for her – but for the relationship that had never been, and for all the babies she had helped to sell, their fates unknown.

As he said goodbye, George shook hands with them both. His fingers lingered slightly on Lucy's, which were warm from stoking the fire.

'Call me Johnny,' he said.

*

Malodorous though the nearby canal was, walking beside it was a peaceful way of winding down after a long day. Parris had mentioned a little community of sorts living on the barges, including the inevitable hard-up artist and one or two hardened cases. Sometimes they caused trouble; and sometimes trouble was caused for them. There was little traffic to disturb their days, apart from one vessel carrying coal that was drawn by a mule.

Near the lock, George reached a ramshackle narrowboat whose grimy windows were obscured by blankets stretched across to serve as crude curtains. They seemed to tremble a little as he passed by.

He paused on the towpath. Being new to Oxford, the other method of transportation out of the city had escaped him.

*

On the outskirts of the capital, Fetch was drawing deep on his pipe in a forlorn-looking pub where nobody asked any questions – except to sell you something.

He had been tempted to head for the big city back in the summer to make himself scarce for a while after all the bloody panic over that stupid little college bint with a dicky heart who'd taken too many Bennies and was found dead in her bed.

Now it was time to disappear into the Smoke for good. He could always lose himself in London, he thought, and he could hardly go back to being a bulldog. Above all, Victor would be glad to have his right-hand man back by his side.

CHAPTER 39

Lewis was sorry to say goodbye to DS George. Presumably they were unlikely to meet again in the ordinary way of things, even in a small place like Oxford. It probably wasn't the done thing to invite a police detective to the pub for a drink; it might get one talked about, which would never do. Yet there was something important that he needed to say to the young man before they parted company.

'Please, I beg of you, do keep my name out of the papers. That's all I ask. I'm sure Oxford's *Mail* and *Times* will be splashing this all over their front pages, but my part in it really must not be mentioned at all. I'm afraid I have my position to consider. I do hope you understand.'

George inclined his head in assent, smiling as they shook hands.

He was as good as his word. When Warnie waved the local newspapers in front of his brother with great excitement at the biggest scandal to hit Oxford for many a year, Lewis was able to feign unworldly donnish ignorance of such a monstrous crime as baby-trafficking. Luckily Minto suspected nothing either.

Lewis had gone round to Alfred's under cover of darkness to beseech father and daughter to keep mum too. Unexpectedly, Lucy had reached forward and pecked him on the cheek. Had it not been florid already, a blush might have been seen.

'You're a dear, Mr Lewis. Of course we will. I've asked DS George to keep our names out of it as well – Dad insisted. We'll let the police take all the credit, and it can be our little secret.'

Lewis smiled down at her steady grey gaze. 'Will you be asked to testify against Edmund Jarvis?'

Lucy looked suddenly bashful. 'Johnny – I mean DS George – has enough evidence against him. Anyway, it might be awkward for me with the OUP – although,' she added, 'that depends on whether I stay there or not.'

Somehow he doubted it. She was probably on course for a life elsewhere. He was hardly a racing man, like his brother, but he could sense the moment when, as Warnie might put it, a filly had the bit between her teeth.

'Please do give my very best regards to Miss Temple,' he said gently. 'We hope to see her back at the university next autumn to resit a year if she wishes. She would be most welcome.'

*

Lewis sent Dorothy a brief letter about Susan's rescue.

The day after it arrived, she was back in Oxford to hear more over a pre-Christmas drink in the Common Room. To his relief, no one looked their way. And, despite several chins wagging in whispered conversations, there were no signs that anyone at Magdalen yet suspected fogeyish old Jack Lewis of any involvement in the scandalous case.

'Narcissism,' said Dorothy. 'It's all down to narcissism, Jack. No empathy for other human beings – just self-obsession. Someone like Ashover would have no feelings towards the unfortunate women in her charge. There would be no point in trying to appeal to her conscience because she has none. Instead, you need to outwit people like her.

'And the more vicious ones like Ashover enjoy inflicting pain on others because of the sense of power it gives them. How else do you think they recruited guards for those ghastly camps during the war? The very worst of human wickedness was given free rein to torment the prisoners.'

'That's a bit strong,' he said, 'comparing those creatures with Ashover. So far as we know, she hasn't killed anyone yet – except, perhaps, their spirit.'

Dorothy shrugged. 'It's a spectrum, Jack, a spectrum.'

Thinking of some of his old schoolteachers at Wynyard (especially the bully of a headmaster) and the fate of the poor tinker boy in Liam Mitchell's class, he couldn't help but agree.

She raised a glass. 'Here's to the study of goodness – and evil. Some of the female fiends can be just as bad as the male ones, so don't get taken in by their wiles.' She smiled slyly at her companion. 'You really should put Ashover in a book, Jack – before I do! I sometimes think,' she added teasingly, 'that you're rather timid around women, my friend.'

CHAPTER 40

Compared with Magdalen, Christ Church was a hotbed of gossip about the baby-trafficking case. With one of its bulldogs on the run from the police, everyone there was wondering what everyone else knew.

Squirrel had finally come good by 'coughing' his inside information over several useful pints at the Perch. 'You want to be very careful, Mr Lewis,' he cautioned.

'But why did the proctors, who are supposed to be in charge, let Fetchley get away with his bullying empire?' persisted his interrogator. 'After all, I understand the senior proctor is such a stickler for rules that he would shop his own grandmother if she walked the wrong way down a street.'

Between gulps, the scout blurted out a name that did not surprise him. Resigned to being an object of envy among other Fellows, Lewis had always tried to not be too cynical. It was, he felt, a stance that corroded the soul. He of all people should try to have faith in the goodness of human nature until proved otherwise.

Yet he had always been suspicious about the over-effusive friendliness shown him by a colleague from the same faculty whenever they passed in the street or the corridor. Not exactly hero-worship – that was for young people or some of his many correspondents – but a trifle squirm-making nonetheless. And also unheard-of. It just wasn't the competitive, academic, chilly English way.

The exception had been the late Charles Williams: not having been an academic in the first place, he was about as full of the milk of human kindness as you could get without actually wearing a dog collar. Yet he had never gushed, unlike Lewis's greeter in the streets. Dash it all, thought the don. I may be taking a risk, but after what Squirrel has told me, I'm going to have to confront the man once and for all so that this business is finally settled.

Unlike every other college in the university, Christ Church had a man of God as its head of house: the dean. The blow to its reputation would be all the more disastrous, thought Lewis, if it didn't bend every effort towards capturing Fetch, mastermind of the illegal supply chain.

After knocking on the Christ Church proctors' office door and putting his head round it without waiting for a reply, he was greeted by the light-green gaze of the ever-affable junior proctor, a smile stitched on his face.

'Mr Lewis, how very nice to see you,' he said immediately.

The senior proctor was nowhere to be seen, and the place had an air of siege about it. The chief clerk, along with his underlings, glowered at this inopportune visitor at such a time of crisis, expecting formality – especially from a member of another college.

Lewis ignored them. If ever there were a moment to pull rank, this was it. 'Do you mind if I take up a little of your time on an academic matter? Shall we take a turn around the quad?' he suggested to the junior proctor.

Safely outside, he staged his second ambush. 'I wonder if you can help me. In truth, my query is not strictly academic, yet of course it concerns us all at the university in the end. This matter of the bulldog Michael Fetchley, who has been causing so much trouble in various loathsome ways, puzzles me. He seemed to have thought he was above the law. Indeed, he has been relying upon other people's silence to get away with it, possibly because he kept them in various supplies they had become accustomed to – even illegal ones.'

Until then, James Slade's bland green gaze had been fixed unwaveringly on Lewis, who was pacing slowly alongside him with his large farmer's hands folded behind his back.

'No doubt you will be aware that the police have sent out search parties for Fetchley, who seems to have fled from Oxford, and any information that people may be able to give will be very useful. I am sure the senior proctor will be grateful for any help in that quarter, poor man – not to mention the dean himself.'

He had hit home: no protestations of indignation that one might reasonably expect from an innocent party.

There was a pause, and then the ever-smiling junior proctor remarked softly and provocatively, 'The college kitchens are certainly going to suffer after this – what howls of complaint there will be about all the shortages.'

'Let them,' said Lewis. 'It will be a lot fairer all round in this little city in future without the black market.'

After doffing the shabby hat that Minto kept urging him to replace, he turned on his heel and left the quad with a feeling he had not experienced since the First World War – of being a target.

*

A few days later, Lewis received a letter forwarded via the usual back-door route of Alfred and Squirrel. The warmth of it surprised and rather touched him.

'Dear Mr Lewis,' wrote Susan. 'I just wanted to say thank you for being such a brick. You have been quite the best friend a girl could ever have, and you've saved my bacon. I am moving to a London hostel very soon to prepare for when the time comes, but please don't worry about me. Lucy will keep you up to date with the details. Peter is going to help me with funds for a while so that my parents don't know I've left Oxford, although, of course, I'll have to tell them sooner or later.

'I just wanted to assure you that I plan to be back next autumn to retake a year. I wouldn't want to miss any of your tutorials and lectures, and I hope we can sometimes meet socially too, if possible. Meanwhile, I know I can rely on your absolute discretion. With all my gratitude, S.'

He placed it carefully within the leaves of a dilapidated book in his Magdalen study, where, he judged, no one would look. Then, on an impulse, he reached inside a drawer for a notebook that had languished there for eight years.

It contained some thoughts about a children's adventure, the writing of which had been interrupted by the outbreak of war, his Home Guard duties, the demands of his academic work and all the other writings, not to mention answering all those fan letters, about which one must never complain but always feel eternally grateful.

He stared at the pages.

The story had been intended for his godchild, Lucy, but only the very beginnings of the tale had been sketched out.

Lucy.

He lit a pipe, looked thoughtfully at his inky fingers and then dipped his pen in the well.

AUTHOR'S NOTE

This is a work of fiction, inspired by some well-established facts. Rake Hall and its illegal activities are entirely my invention, but a building that was once a mother-and-baby home still exists in central Oxford. My mother stayed there for three months while pregnant with me.

There is no evidence that any UK mother-and-baby hostels were ever involved in the crime of baby-trafficking. However, it was a significant enough real-life problem to be flagged up by *John Bull* magazine as early as 4 June 1932 in an article headlined 'Stamp Out Our Baby Sellers!'

The post-war Ghost Squad was a well-documented police under-cover operation, though only in London; and photographs reveal that C.S. Lewis did indeed bear a striking resemblance to one of its leading lights, Detective Inspector (later Superintendent) John Gosling. I also drew on Lewis's military service in the First World

War and the Second World War's Home Guard to emphasise that he would be familiar with weapons as a fictional crime-fighter in my novel.

Apart from Mrs 'Minto' Moore, Lewis's brother Warren (Warnie) and Lewis's writer friend Dorothy L. Sayers, his Inklings friends J.R.R. (John) Tolkien, Owen Barfield and Charles Williams, and DI John Gosling, all my other characters are fictional.

Readers interested in learning more about C.S. Lewis are referred to the several excellent biographies of his life as well as to his own writings. Although this book is my version of 'Jack' Lewis, I have endeavoured to make an imagined collision in post-war Oxford between two different worlds plausible on its own terms.

ACKNOWLEDGEMENTS

My thanks to my wonderful Swift Press publisher and co-founder Mark Richards for all his enthusiasm and advice as well as to Swift's managing director and co-founder Diana Broccardo, managing editor Lucie Ewin and marketing and publicity director Rachel Nobilo. I'm also very grateful to publicity consultant Emma Harrow for her PR expertise and to editors Luke Brown and Liz Hudson for their advice and encouragement.

My former non-fiction agent Judith Chilcote told me back in 2000 that I should write fiction one day. Well, Judy, I've got there at long last. The crime novelists T.P. Fielden (Christopher Wilson) and Alice Castle as well as the editor and writer Corinna Honan kindly gave me invaluable advice, while my academic friends Victoria Neumark Jones (who shared her Oxford University experiences, especially in non-couture gowns) and Barbara Rowlands have been great cheerleaders along the journey. Thanks are also due to Vanessa Holt for boosting my confidence early on by telling me that she loved the book. And a final tribute should be paid to my very patient civil partner Norman Jopling, who believed in this project from the start.

FURTHER READING

Carpenter, Humphrey, *The Inklings* (London: Allen & Unwin, 1978).

Davies, Hunter, *The Co-op's Got Bananas!* (London: Simon & Schuster, 2016).

Dent, Alan C., An Oxford Policeman's Lot 1948–1973, www.headington.org.uk/history/dent

Gosling, John, *The Ghost Squad* (London: Panther, 1961).

Hannay, Margaret, 'Surprised by Joy: C.S. Lewis's Changing Attitude Towards Women', in *Mythlore: A Journal of J.R.R. Tolkien, C.S. Lewis, Charles Williams and Mythopoeic Literature*, vol. 4, no. 1, Article 5.

Horobin, Simon, *C.S. Lewis's Oxford* (Oxford: Bodleian Publishing, 2024).

Jackson, Ashley, *Oxford's War 1939–1945* (Oxford Bodleian Publishing, 2024)

Kirby, Dick, *Scotland Yard's Ghost Squad* (Barnsley: Pen & Sword, 2011).

Langrish, Katherine, *From Spare Oom to War Drobe* (London: Darton, Longman & Todd, 2021).

Larkin, Philip, *Jill* (London: Faber & Faber, 1946).

Lewis, C.S., *The Allegory of Love* (Oxford: Oxford University Press, 1936).

—— *The Screwtape Letters* (London: Geoffrey Bles, 1942).

—— *That Hideous Strength* (London: John Lane, The Bodley Head, 1945)

—— *The Lion, the Witch and the Wardrobe* (London: Geoffrey Bles, 1950).

Milotte, Mike, *Abandoned Babies: The Secret History of Ireland's Baby Export Business* (Dublin: New Island Books, 1997).

Patten, Marguerite, *Post-war Kitchen: Nostalgic Food and Facts from 1945–1954* (London: Hamlyn, 1998).

Platt, Christopher, *The Most Obliging Man in Europe: Life and Times of the Oxford Scout* (London: Allen & Unwin, 1986).

Reynolds, Barbara, Dorothy L. Sayers, *Her Life and Soul* (London: Sceptre, 1994).

Sayer, George, *Jack: A Life of C.S. Lewis* (London: Hodder & Stoughton, 1997).

Sayers, Dorothy L., *Gaudy Night* (London: Victor Gollancz, 1935).

Sullivan, Paul, *The Secret History of Oxford* (Stroud: The History Press, 2013).

Waller, Maureen, *London 1945* (London: John Murray, 2004).

Ward, Michael, *Planet Narnia* (Oxford: Oxford University Press, 2008).

Whitehorn, Katharine, *Selective Memory* (London: Virago, 2007).

Wilson, A. N., *C.S. Lewis: A Biography* (London: Collins, 1990).

Wyatt, Will, *Oxford Boy: A Post-war Townie Childhood* (Oxford: Signal Books, 2018).